PENGUIN POPULAR CLASSICS

HAMLET
BY WILLIAM SHAKESPEARE

PENGUIN POPULAR CLASSICS

HAMLET

WILLIAM SHAKESPEARE

PENGUIN BOOKS
A PENGUIN/GODFREY CAVE EDITION

PENGUIN BOOKS

Published by the Penguin Group
Penguin Books Ltd, 27 Wrights Lane, London w8 5tz, England
Penguin Books USA Inc., 375 Hudson Street, New York, New York 10014, USA
Penguin Books Australia Ltd, Ringwood, Victoria, Australia
Penguin Books Canada Ltd, 10 Alcorn Avenue, Toronto, Ontario, Canada m4v 3b2
Penguin Books (NZ) Ltd, 182–190 Wairau Road, Auckland 10, New Zealand

Penguin Books Ltd, Registered Offices: Harmondsworth, Middlesex, England

Published in Penguin Popular Classics 1994

3 5 7 9 10 8 6 4 2

Printed in England by Clays Ltd, St Ives plc

CONTENTS

The Works of Shakespeare   6

William Shakespeare   7

The Elizabethan Theatre   11

The Globe Theatre   13

The Tragedy of Hamlet (Introduction)   15

THE TRAGEDY OF HAMLET,
    PRINCE OF DENMARK   23

Notes   157

Glossary   185

THE WORKS OF SHAKESPEARE

APPROXIMATE DATE | PLAYS | FIRST PRINTED

Before 1594
- HENRY VI *three parts* — Folio 1623
- RICHARD III — 1597
- TITUS ANDRONICUS — 1594
- LOVE'S LABOUR'S LOST — 1598
- THE TWO GENTLEMEN OF VERONA — Folio
- THE COMEDY OF ERRORS — Folio
- THE TAMING OF THE SHREW — Folio

1594–1597
- ROMEO AND JULIET (*pirated* 1597) — 1599
- A MIDSUMMER NIGHT'S DREAM — 1600
- RICHARD II — 1597
- KING JOHN — Folio
- THE MERCHANT OF VENICE — 1600

1597–1600
- HENRY IV *part i* — 1598
- HENRY IV *part ii* — 1600
- HENRY V (*pirated* 1600) — Folio
- MUCH ADO ABOUT NOTHING — 1600
- MERRY WIVES OF WINDSOR (*pirated* 1602) — Folio
- AS YOU LIKE IT — Folio
- JULIUS CAESAR — Folio
- TROYLUS AND CRESSIDA — 1609

1601–1608
- HAMLET (*pirated* 1603) — 1604
- TWELFTH NIGHT — Folio
- MEASURE FOR MEASURE — Folio
- ALL'S WELL THAT ENDS WELL — Folio
- OTHELLO — 1622
- LEAR — 1608
- MACBETH — Folio
- TIMON OF ATHENS — Folio
- ANTONY AND CLEOPATRA — Folio
- CORIOLANUS — Folio

After 1608
- PERICLES (*omitted from the Folio*) — 1609
- CYMBELINE — Folio
- THE WINTER'S TALE — Folio
- THE TEMPEST — Folio
- HENRY VIII — Folio

POEMS

DATES UNKNOWN
- VENUS AND ADONIS — 1593
- THE RAPE OF LUCRECE — 1594
- SONNETS ⎱
- A LOVER'S COMPLAINT ⎰ — 1609
- THE PHOENIX AND THE TURTLE — 1601

WILLIAM SHAKESPEARE

William Shakespeare was born at Stratford upon Avon in April, 1564. He was the third child, and eldest son, of John Shakespeare and Mary Arden. His father was one of the most prosperous men of Stratford, who held in turn the chief offices in the town. His mother was of gentle birth, the daughter of Robert Arden of Wilmcote. In December, 1582, Shakespeare married Ann Hathaway, daughter of a farmer of Shottery, near Stratford; their first child Susanna was baptized on May 6, 1583, and twins, Hamnet and Judith, on February 22, 1585. Little is known of Shakespeare's early life; but it is unlikely that a writer who dramatized such an incomparable range and variety of human kinds and experiences should have spent his early manhood entirely in placid pursuits in a country town. There is one tradition, not universally accepted, that he fled from Stratford because he was in trouble for deer stealing, and had fallen foul of Sir Thomas Lucy, the local magnate; another that he was for some time a schoolmaster.

From 1592 onwards the records are much fuller. In March, 1592, the Lord Strange's players produced a new play at the Rose Theatre called *Harry the Sixth*, which was very successful, and was probably the *First Part of Henry VI*. In the autumn of 1592 Robert Greene, the best known of the professional writers, as he was dying wrote a letter to three fellow writers in which he warned them against the ingratitude of players in general, and in particular against an 'upstart crow' who 'supposes he is as much able to bombast out a blank verse as the best of you: and being an absolute Johannes Factotum is in his own conceit the only

Shake-scene in a country.' This is the first reference to Shakespeare, and the whole passage suggests that Shakespeare had become suddenly famous as a playwright. At this time Shakespeare was brought into touch with Edward Alleyne the great tragedian, and Christopher Marlowe, whose thundering parts of Tamburlaine, the Jew of Malta, and Dr. Faustus Alleyne was acting, as well as Hieronimo, the hero of Kyd's *Spanish Tragedy*, the most famous of all Elizabethan plays.

In April, 1593, Shakespeare published his poem *Venus and Adonis*, which was dedicated to the young Earl of Southampton: it was a great and lasting success, and was reprinted nine times in the next few years. In May, 1594, his second poem, *The Rape of Lucrece*, was also dedicated to Southampton.

There was little playing in 1593, for the theatres were shut during a severe outbreak of the plague; but in the autumn of 1594, when the plague ceased, the playing companies were reorganized, and Shakespeare became a sharer in the Lord Chamberlain's company who went to play in the Theatre in Shoreditch. During these months Marlowe and Kyd had died. Shakespeare was thus for a time without a rival. He had already written the three parts of *Henry VI*, *Richard III*, *Titus Andronicus*, *The Two Gentlemen of Verona*, *Love's Labour's Lost*, *The Comedy of Errors*, and *The Taming of the Shrew*. Soon afterwards he wrote the first of his greater plays – *Romeo and Juliet* – and he followed this success in the next three years with *A Midsummer Night's Dream*, *Richard II*, and *The Merchant of Venice*, The two parts of *Henry IV*, introducing Falstaff, the most popular of all his comic characters, were written in 1597–8.

The company left the Theatre in 1597 owing to disputes over a renewal of the ground lease, and went to play at the

Curtain in the same neighbourhood. The disputes continued throughout 1598, and at Christmas the players settled the matter by demolishing the old Theatre and re-erecting a new playhouse on the South bank of the Thames, near Southwark Cathedral. This playhouse was named the Globe. The expenses of the new building were shared by the chief members of the Company, including Shakespeare, who was now a man of some means. In 1596 he had bought New Place, a large house in the centre of Stratford, for £60, and through his father purchased a coat-of-arms from the Heralds, which was the official recognition that he and his family were gentlefolk.

By the summer of 1598 Shakespeare was recognized as the greatest of English dramatists. Booksellers were printing his more popular plays, at times even in pirated or stolen versions, and he received a remarkable tribute from a young writer named Francis Meres, in his book *Palladis Tamia*. In a long catalogue of English authors Meres gave Shakespeare more prominence than any other writer, and mentioned by name twelve of his plays.

Shortly before the Globe was opened, Shakespeare had completed the cycle of plays dealing with the whole story of the Wars of the Roses with *Henry V*. It was followed by *As You Like It*, and *Julius Caesar*, the first of the maturer tragedies. In the next three years he wrote *Troylus and Cressida*, *The Merry Wives of Windsor*, *Hamlet*, and *Twelfth Night*.

On March 24, 1603, Queen Elizabeth I died. The company had often performed before her, but they found her successor a far more enthusiastic patron. One of the first acts of King James was to take over the company and to promote them to be his own servants, so that henceforward they were known as the King's Men. They acted now very frequently at Court, and prospered accordingly. In the early years of the reign Shakespeare wrote the more sombre comedies, *All's Well that Ends Well,* and *Measure for Measure,* which were followed by *Othello, Macbeth,* and *King Lear.* Then he returned to Roman themes with *Antony and Cleopatra* and *Coriolanus.*

Since 1601 Shakespeare had been writing less, and there were now a number of rival dramatists who were introducing new styles of drama, particularly Ben Jonson (whose first successful comedy, *Every Man in his Humour,* was acted by Shakespeare's company in 1598), Chapman, Dekker, Marston, and Beaumont and Fletcher who began to write in 1607. In 1608 the King's Men acquired a second playhouse, an indoor private theatre in the fashionable quarter of the Blackfriars. At private theatres, plays were performed indoors; the prices charged were higher than in the public playhouses, and the audience consequently was more select. Shakespeare seems to have retired from the stage about this time: his name does not occur in the various lists of players after 1607. Henceforward he lived for the most part at Stratford, where he was regarded as one of the most important citizens. He still wrote a few plays, and he tried his hand at the new form of tragi-comedy – a play with tragic incidents but a happy ending – which Beaumont and Fletcher had popularized. He wrote four of these – *Pericles, Cymbeline, The Winter's Tale,* and *The Tempest,* which was acted at Court in 1611. For the last four years of his life he lived in retirement. His son Hamnet had died in 1596: his two daughters were now married. Shakespeare died at Stratford upon Avon on April 23, 1616, and was buried in the chancel of the church, before the high altar. Shortly afterwards a memorial which still exists, with a portrait bust, was set up on the North wall. His wife survived him.

When Shakespeare died fourteen of his plays had been separately published in Quarto booklets. In 1623 his surviving fellow actors, John Heming and Henry Condell, with the co-operation of a number of printers, published a collected edition of thirty-six plays in one Folio volume, with an engraved portrait, memorial verses by Ben Jonson and others, and an Epistle to the Reader in which Heming and Condell make the interesting note that Shakespeare's 'hand and mind went together, and what he thought, he uttered with that easiness that we have scarce received from him a blot in his papers'.

The plays as printed in the Quartos or the Folio differ considerably from the usual modern text. They are often not divided into scenes, and sometimes not even into acts. Nor are there place-headings at the beginning of each scene, because in the Elizabethan theatre there was no scenery. They are carelessly printed and the spelling is erratic.

THE ELIZABETHAN THEATRE

Although plays of one sort and another had been acted for many generations, no permanent playhouse was erected in England until 1576. In the 1570s the Lord Mayor and Aldermen of the City of London and the players were constantly at variance. As a result James Burbage, then the leader of the great Earl of Leicester's players, decided that he would erect a playhouse outside the jurisdiction of the Lord Mayor, where the players would no longer be hindered by the authorities. Accordingly in 1576 he built the Theatre in Shoreditch, at that time a suburb of London. The experiment was successful, and by 1592 there were two more playhouses in London, the Curtain (also in Shoreditch), and the Rose on the south bank of the river, near Southwark Cathedral.

Elizabethan players were accustomed to act on a variety of stages; in the great hall of a nobleman's house, or one of the Queen's palaces, in town halls and in yards, as well as their own theatre.

The public playhouse for which most of Shakespeare's plays were written was a small and intimate affair. The outside measurement of the Fortune Theatre, which was built in 1600 to rival the new Globe, was but eighty feet square. Playhouses were usually circular or octagonal, with three tiers of galleries looking down upon the yard or pit, which was open to the sky. The stage jutted out into the yard so that the actors came forward into the midst of their audience.

Over the stage there was a roof, and on either side doors by which the characters entered or disappeared. Over the back of the stage ran a gallery or upper stage which was used whenever an upper scene was needed, as when Romeo climbs up to Juliet's bedroom, or the citizens of Angiers address King John from the walls. The space beneath this upper stage was known as the tiring house; it was concealed from the audience by a curtain which would be drawn back to reveal an inner stage, for such scenes as the witches' cave in *Macbeth,* Prospero's cell, or Juliet's tomb.

There was no general curtain concealing the whole stage, so that all scenes on the main stage began with an entrance and ended with an exit. Thus in tragedies the dead must be carried away. There was no scenery, and therefore no limit to the number of scenes, for a scene came to an end when the characters left the stage. When it was necessary for the exact locality of a scene to be known, then Shakespeare

THE GLOBE THEATRE

Wood–engraving by R. J. Beedham after a reconstruction by J. C. Adams

indicated it in the dialogue; otherwise a simple property or a garment was sufficient; a chair or still showed an indoor scene, a man wearing riding boots was a messenger, a king wearing armour was on the battlefield, or the like. Such simplicity was on the whole an advantage; the spectator was not distracted by the setting and Shakespeare was able to use as many scenes as he wished. The action passed by very quickly: a play of 2500 lines of verse could be acted in two hours. Moreover, since the actor was so close to his audience, the slightest subtlety of voice and gesture was easily appreciated.

The company was a 'Fellowship of Players', who were all partners and sharers. There were usually ten to fifteen full members, with three or four boys, and some paid servants. Shakespeare had therefore to write for his team. The chief actor in the company was Richard Burbage, who first distinguished himself as Richard III; for him Shakespeare wrote his great tragic parts. An important member of the company was the clown or low comedian. From 1594 to 1600 the company's clown was Will Kemp; he was succeeded by Robert Armin. No women were allowed to appear on the stage, and all women's parts were taken by boys.

*

THE TRAGEDY OF HAMLET

Hamlet was written between 1598 and the summer of 1602, and probably during the winter of 1601-2.

It was a time of great troubles, some of which are reflected in the play itself. In February, 1601, the Earl of Essex, who was universally regarded as a national hero, after sixteen months' political exile from Court made his futile rebellion and was executed. His death caused vast gloom and a general feeling of cynical disillusion, which is reflected in many plays and books. During these months also the Stage War, in which Ben Jonson and John Marston, writing for two rival companies of Children, had attacked each other in successive plays, came to a head in the autumn of 1601, when Ben Jonson's attempt to crush his opponents in *Poetaster* was derisively countered by Dekker's *Satiromastix*, which Shakespeare's company put on. At Christmas, 1601, English troops, who were sharing in the defence of Ostend under the command of Sir Francis Vere, achieved a brilliant victory against enormous odds. There are references to the first two, and probably to the third of these events in the play. These and other echoes of contemporary feeling are recorded in the notes.

The story of *Hamlet* in some form is found very early in European literature. It occurs in the *Historia Danica* of Saxo Grammaticus, who flourished about A.D. 1250, but the immediate source of the play is in the *Histoires Tragiques* of François de Belleforest, published in Paris in 1570. Belleforest's story is crude and bloody. It tells how in pre-Christian times Prince Horvendile, father of Hamlet, was

murdered by his brother Fengon, who thereupon made an
incestuous marriage with his wife, Queen Geruth. Hamlet,
to escape the tyranny of his uncle, pretended to be mad. To
test his madness, Fengon first caused him to be tempted by
a harlot, but Hamlet, being warned of his danger, escaped.
Next Fengon sent one of his councillors to hide secretly in
the Queen's chamber behind the arras that he might over-
hear Hamlet's conversation with his mother. Hamlet, after
his accustomed manner, crying like a cock, and as it were
beating with his arms upon the hangings, perceived the
listener. Having slain him with his sword, he cut the body
in pieces, which he boiled, and then deposited in the moat
through the privy, for the hogs to eat. Fengon now plotted
to send Hamlet to the King of England with secret letters to
have him put to death. On the voyage Hamlet read the
letters, and substituted others ordering that the messengers
should be hanged, and he himself married to the English
King's daughter, which was accomplished. So Hamlet came
back into Denmark to find that his death was being celebrated in a funeral feast. He waited until the guests were
dead drunk, and then set fire to the hall and destroyed them.
Next he went up to his uncle's bed chamber and cut off his
head. He now threw off all pretence of being mad. He
made an oration to the Danes to tell them the whole story,
at which they were so greatly moved that they proclaimed
him King. After his coronation he went back into England,
where the King would have murdered him, but he escaped.
When he did return to Denmark it was with two wives, for
the Queen of the Scots, being somewhat of an Amazon,
had fallen in love with him, and insisted on marrying him.
This second wife, whose name was Hermetrude, soon
proved disloyal. She fell in love with Wiglerus, his uncle,
and Hamlet was treacherously slain.

This story was the basis of a play which was produced some time before 1589.

In 1589 Thomas Nashe, who was then a bright young man, wrote a preface for Greene's novel, *Menaphon*, in which he mocked various writers of the time. Amongst other remarks he observed: 'It is a common practice nowadays amongst a sort of shifting companions, that run through every art and thrive by none, to leave the trade of *Noverint* whereto they were born, and busy themselves with the endeavours of Art, that could scarcely latinize their neck-verse if they should have need; yet English Seneca read by candle-light yields many good sentences as "Blood is a beggar", and so forth: and if you intreat him fair in a frosty morning, he will afford you whole *Hamlets*, I should say handfuls of tragical speeches.' These remarks, and those which follow, suggest that 'English Seneca' was probably Thomas Kyd, the author of the *Spanish Tragedy*, the most famous and popular of all Elizabethan tragedies. The *Spanish Tragedy* told how old Hieronimo took vengeance on the murders of his son Horatio.

Between 1592 and 1594 there were severe outbreaks of the plague, and little playing was possible in London, but in June, 1594, the players of the two leading companies, the Lord Chámberlain's and the Admiral's, amalgamated for a few days to perform in a small theatre in Newington Butts, and amongst the plays then acted was *Hamlet*, performed on the 9th June.

There is another reference to *Hamlet* in 1596, when Thomas Lodge wrote a curious book called *Wit's Misery and the World's Madness* in which he described allegorically various contemporary types. The way to know the Devil, Hate-Virtue, he said, was by this: 'He walks for the most part in black under colour of gravity, and looks as pale as the visard of the ghost which cried so miserably at the Theatre like an oyster wife, *Hamlet, revenge.*'

There was therefore a *Hamlet* play in existence and popular between 1589 and 1596. Whether written by Kyd or not, it was produced during Kyd's lifetime, and it had affinities with the *Spanish Tragedy*. It is not likely that Shakespeare's play as now known was written before 1598, for the style is too mature for it to have been one of his early works. This earlier *Hamlet* has disappeared, but there is a crude German version known as *Bestrafte Brudermord*, or *Fratricide Punished*.

The known history of Shakespeare's play begins in 1602. On the 26th July James Roberts, a printer, entered in the Stationers' Register, a book called 'The Revenge of Hamlet, Prince of Denmark, as it was lately acted by the Lord Chamberlain, his servants.' This entry was apparently intended to block publication. From time to time the players persuaded Roberts to enter one of their books, and so secure the sole right to print it in order that the book might not be issued by any other printer. There was, however, no intention that anyone should print it.

In 1603 there appeared the first version of Shakespeare's *Hamlet*. This is known as the FIRST QUARTO. The title-page runs: *The Tragicall Historie of HAMLET Prince of Denmarke. By William Shakespeare. As it hath been diverse times acted by his Highness' servants in the City of London: as also in the two Universities of Cambridge and Oxford, and elsewhere.* The fact that the Company are called 'his Highness' Servants' shows that the Quarto was issued after 19th May, when King James adopted the former Lord Chamberlain's Men as his own company.

The First Quarto is a very garbled version of Shakespeare's play and not printed from any authorized manuscript. By

1603 Shakespeare's plays were valuable to printers, and even so bad a version was worth printing. It is very much shorter than the true play, and differs in a number of details. The old councillor appears as Corambis, not Polonius, and the arrangements of the scenes are different. More than 240 lines in the First Quarto do not appear in any form in the other versions. Parts of the play certainly seem to have been taken down in shorthand by a reporter who was not very expert. Thus he reproduces Hamlet's speech after the departure of the Ghost (p. 51, l. 12) as follows:

> O all you host of heaven! O earth, what else?
> And shall I couple hell; remember thee?
> Yes thou poor Ghost; from the tables
> Of my memory, I'll wipe away all saws of books,
> All trivial fond conceits
> That ever youth, or else observance noted,
> And thy remembrance all alone shall sit.
> Yes, yes, by heaven, a damned pernicious villain,
> Murderous, bawdy, smiling damned villain,
> (My tables) meet it is I set it down,
> That one may smile, and smile, and be a villain;
> At least I am sure, it may be so in Denmark.
> So uncle, there you are, there you are.
> Now to the words; it is adieu adieu: remember me,
> So 'tis enough, I have sworn.

Various differing theories have been offered to explain how this Quarto was compiled, but it is generally agreed that it is in part at least a report of an actual performance. It has little value as a text, but some of the stage directions, recording what the reporter saw at a performance, are most interesting. It may possibly represent a version of the play in a transition stage, before Shakespeare had completely rewritten the old *Hamlet*.

In the following year, 1604, a new edition of the play came out. This is known as the SECOND QUARTO. Its title page runs: *The Tragicall Historie of HAMLET, Prince of Denmark. By William Shakespeare. Newly imprinted and enlarged to almost as much again as it was, according to the true and perfect Coppie.* This Second Quarto gives the completest text of the play. It was probably set up direct from Shakespeare's manuscript, but if so, by a careless printer, who made many blunders. This Second Quarto was reprinted in 1607 and 1611.

When the play was printed in its place in the FIRST FOLIO of 1623 the text was again different. A number of passages in the Quarto were omitted, and a few passages which do not occur in the Quarto were included. The Folio although shorter is, on the whole, a better text than the Quarto. Speeches generally have been more carefully punctuated, and many of the mis-readings in the Quarto are given correctly. On the other hand, the Folio has many mistakes of its own. In the Quarto neither Acts nor Scenes are marked: in the Folio Acts and Scenes are marked down to the beginning of II, ii but not afterwards. The general opinion held by modern scholars is that the Folio was set up from a copy of the playhouse copy. The copyist, whoever he was, varied in his care. Sometimes he gave a good version, sometimes he was extremely careless. Neither Second Quarto nor Folio by itself is reliable.

The problems of the text of *Hamlet* are thus complex, highly controversial, and insoluble; an editor must compromise if he is to produce a readable text. In the nineteenth century it was usual to compound a text from the Second

Quarto and Folio, selecting those readings which in the editor's opinion appeared most desirable. More recently, editors have preferred the Second Quarto as a basis for their text, correcting obvious mis-readings by the Folio. I have, however, preferred the Folio, because whilst the Quarto doubtless represents Shakespeare's play as first written, the Folio is nearer to the play as acted, and it is probable that Shakespeare himself was responsible for some of the alterations and different readings. At the same time, where the Folio seems obviously to have gone wrong, the better Quarto readings have been adopted, and those passages in the Quarto not printed in the Folio have been included, but marked with [ ]. The reader can thus see how the play was cut for acting.

In this edition the principles adopted in the other volumes have been followed. Spelling has been modernized, but the general arrangement and the punctuation, which 'points' the text for reading aloud, have for the most part been left. The reader who is used to the 'accepted' text may thus find certain unfamiliarities, but the text itself is nearer to that used in Shakespeare's own playhouse.

The Tragedy of Hamlet,
Prince of Denmark

THE ACTORS' NAMES

CLAUDIUS, King of Denmark
HAMLET, son to the late, and nephew to the present King
POLONIUS, Lord Chamberlain
HORATIO, friend to Hamlet
LAERTES, son of Polonius
VOLTEMAND,
CORNELIUS,
ROSENCRANTZ,
GUILDENSTERN, } courtiers
OSRIC,
A GENTLEMAN,
A PRIEST
MARCELLUS,
BARNARDO, } soldiers
FRANCISCO,
REYNALDO, servant to Polonius
The Players
Two Clowns, grave-diggers
FORTINBRAS, Prince of Norway
A Captain
English Ambassadors
GERTRUDE, Queen of Denmark, and mother to Hamlet
OPHELIA, daughter to Polonius
GHOST of Hamlet's Father

I.1

Enter Bernardo and Francisco, two sentinels.

BARNARDO: Who's there?

FRANCISCO: Nay answer me. Stand and unfold yourself.

BARNARDO: Long live the King.

FRANCISCO: Barnardo?

BARNARDO: He.

FRANCISCO: You come most carefully upon your hour.

BARNARDO: 'Tis now struck twelve, get thee to bed
Francisco.

FRANCISCO: For this relief much thanks: 'tis bitter cold,
And I am sick at heart.

BARNARDO: Have you had quiet guard?

FRANCISCO: Not a mouse stirring.

BARNARDO: Well, good night.
If you do meet Horatio and Marcellus,
The rivals of my watch, bid them make haste.

Enter Horatio and Marcellus.

FRANCISCO: I think I hear them. Stand: ho, who is there?

HORATIO: Friends to this ground.

MARCELLUS: And liegemen to the Dane.

FRANCISCO: Give you good night.

MARCELLUS: O, farewell honest soldiers, who hath
reliev'd you?

FRANCISCO: Barnardo has my place: give you good
night.

Exit Francisco.

MARCELLUS: Holla Barnardo.

BARNARDO: Say, what is Horatio there?

HORATIO: A piece of him.

BARNARDO: Welcome Horatio, welcome good Marcellus.
MARCELLUS: What, has this thing appear'd again to-night?
BARNARDO: I have seen nothing.
MARCELLUS: Horatio says, 'tis but our fantasy,
  And will not let belief take hold of him
  Touching this dreaded sight, twice seen of us;
  Therefore I have entreated him along
  With us, to watch the minutes of this night,
  That if again this apparition come,
  He may approve our eyes, and speak to it.
HORATIO: Tush, tush, 'twill not appear.
BARNARDO: Sit down awhile,
  And let us once again assail your ears,
  That are so fortified against our story,
  What we two nights have seen.
HORATIO: Well, sit we down,
  And let us hear Barnardo speak of this.
BARNARDO: Last night of all,
  When yond same star that's westward from the pole
  Had made his course t' illume that part of heaven
  Where now it burns, Marcellus and myself,
  The bell then beating one –
MARCELLUS: Peace, break thee off:

Enter Ghost.

  Look where it comes again.
BARNARDO: In the same figure, like the King that's dead.
MARCELLUS: Thou art a scholar, speak to it Horatio.
BARNARDO: Looks it not like the King? Mark it Horatio.
HORATIO: Most like: it harrows me with fear and wonder.
BARNARDO: It would be spoke to.
MARCELLUS: Question it Horatio.
HORATIO: What art thou that usurp'st this time of night,
  Together with that fair and warlike form

In which the Majesty of buried Denmark
Did sometimes march: by heaven I charge thee speak.

MARCELLUS: It is offended.

BARNARDO: See, it stalks away.

HORATIO: Stay, speak; speak: I charge thee, speak.

Exit the Ghost.

MARCELLUS: 'Tis gone, and will not answer.

BARNARDO: How now Horatio? you tremble and look
pale:
Is not this something more than fantasy?
What think you on't?

HORATIO: Before my God, I might not this believe
Without the sensible and true avouch
Of mine own eyes.

MARCELLUS: Is it not like the King?

HORATIO: As thou art to thyself,
Such was the very armour he had on,
When he th' ambitious Norway combated:
So frown'd he once, when in an angry parle
He smote the sledded poleaxe on the ice.
'Tis strange.

MARCELLUS: Thus twice before, and jump at this dead
hour,
With martial stalk, hath he gone by our watch.

HORATIO: In what particular thought to work, I know
not:
But in the gross and scope of my opinion,
This bodes some strange eruption to our State.

MARCELLUS: Good now sit down, and tell me he that
knows
Why this same strict and most observant watch,
So nightly toils the subject of the land,
And why such daily cast of brazen cannon

And foreign mart for implements of war:
Why such impress of shipwrights, whose sore task
Does not divide the Sunday from the week,
What might be toward, that this sweaty haste
Doth make the night joint-labourer with the day:
Who is't that can inform me?

HORATIO: That can I,
At least the whisper goes so: our last King,
Whose image even but now appear'd to us,
Was (as you know) by Fortinbras of Norway,
(Thereto prick'd on by a most emulate pride)
Dar'd to the combat. In which, our valiant Hamlet,
(For so this side of our known world esteem'd him)
Did slay this Fortinbras: who by a seal'd compact,
Well ratified by law, and heraldry,
Did forfeit (with his life) all those his lands
Which he stood siez'd of, to the conqueror:
Against the which, a moiety competent
Was gaged by our King: which had return'd
To the inheritance of Fortinbras,
Had he been vanquisher, as by the same cov'nant
And carriage of the article design'd ,
His fell to Hamlet. Now sir, young Fortinbras,
Of unimproved mettle, hot and full
Hath in the skirts of Norway, here and there,
Shark'd up a list of landless resolutes,
For food and diet, to some enterprise
That hath a stomach in't: which is no other
(As it doth well appear unto our state)
But to recover of us by strong hand
And terms compulsative, those foresaid lands
So by his father lost: and this (I take it)
Is the main motive of our preparations,

The source of this our watch, and the chief head
Of this post haste, and romage in the land.
[BARNARDO; I think it be no other, but e'en so;
  Well may it sort that this portentous figure
  Comes armed through our watch so like the King
  That was and is the question of these wars.
HORATIO: A moth it is to trouble the mind's eye:
  In the most high and palmy state of Rome,
  A little ere the mightiest Julius fell,
  The graves stood tenantless, and the sheeted dead
  Did squeak and gibber in the Roman streets;
  As stars with trains of fire and dews of blood,
  Disasters in the sun; and the moist star,
  Upon whose influence Neptune's empire stands,
  Was sick almost to doomsday with eclipse.
  And even the like precurse of fierce events,
  As harbingers preceding still the fates
  And prologue to the omen coming on,
  Have heaven and earth together demonstrated
  Unto our climatures and countrymen.]
                Enter Ghost again.
But soft, behold: lo, where it comes again:
I'll cross it, though it blast me. Stay illusion:
                Ghost spreads his arms.
If thou hast any sound, or use of voice,
Speak to me.
If there be any good thing to be done,
That may to thee do ease, and grace to me:
Speak to me.
If thou art privy to thy country's fate
(Which happily foreknowing may avoid)
O speak.
Or, if thou hast uphoarded in thy life

Extorted treasure in the womb of earth,
(For which, they say, you spirits oft walk in death)
                    The Cock crows.

Speak of it.   Stay, and speak. Stop it Marcellus.

MARCELLUS: Shall I strike at it with my partisan?

HORATIO: Do, if it will not stand.

BARNARDO: 'Tis here.

HORATIO: 'Tis here.
                    Exit Ghost.

MARCELLUS: 'Tis gone.
    We do it wrong, being so majestical
    To offer it the show of violence,
    For it is as the air, invulnerable,
    And our vain blows, malicious mockery.

BARNARDO: It was about to speak, when the cock crew.

HORATIO: And then it started, like a guilty thing
    Upon a fearful summons. I have heard,
    The cock that is the trumpet to the morn,
    Doth with his lofty and shrill-sounding throat
    Awake the god of day: and at his warning,
    Whether in sea, or fire, in earth, or air,
    Th' extravagant, and erring spirit, hies
    To his confine: and of the truth herein,
    This present object made probation.

MARCELLUS: It faded on the crowing of the cock.
    Some say, that ever 'gainst that season comes
    Wherein our Saviour's birth is celebrated,
    The bird of dawning singeth all night long:
    And then (they say) no spirit can walk abroad,
    The nights are wholesome, then no planets strike,
    No fairy takes, nor witch hath power to charm:
    So hallow'd, and so gracious is the time.

HORATIO: So have I heard, and do in part believe it.

But look, the morn in russet mantle clad,
Walks o'er the dew of yon high eastern hill;
Break we our watch up, and by my advice
Let us impart what we have seen to-night
Unto young Hamlet. For upon my life,
This spirit dumb to us will speak to him:
Do you consent we shall acquaint him with it,
As needful in our loves, fitting our duty?
MARCELLUS: Let's do't I pray, and I this morning know
Where we shall find him most conveniently.
Exeunt.

I.2

*Flourish. Enter Claudius, King of Denmark, Gertrude, the
Queen; Council, as Polonius, and his son, Laertes, Hamlet and
others.*

KING: Though yet of Hamlet our dear brother's death
The memory be green: and that it us befitted
To bear our hearts in grief, and our whole Kingdom
To be contracted in one brow of woe:
Yet so far hath discretion fought with nature,
That we with wisest sorrow think on him,
Together with remembrance of ourselves.
Therefore our sometimes sister, now our Queen,
Th' imperial jointress to this warlike State,
Have we, as 'twere, with a defeated joy,
With one auspicious, and one dropping eye,
With mirth in funeral, and with dirge in marriage,
In equal scale weighing delight and dole
Taken to wife; nor have we herein barr'd
Your better wisdoms, which have freely gone
With this affair along, for all our thanks.

Now follows, that you know young Fortinbras,
Holding a weak supposal of our worth;
Or thinking by our late dear Brother's death
Our State to be disjoint, and out of frame,
Colleagued with the dream of his advantage;
He hath not fail'd to pester us with message,
Importing the surrender of those lands
Lost by his father, with all bonds of law
To our most valiant brother: so much for him.
      Enter Voltemand and Cornelius.
Now for ourself, and for this time of meeting,
Thus much the business is. We have here writ
To Norway, uncle of young Fortinbras,
Who impotent and bed-rid, scarcely hears
Of this his nephew's purpose, to suppress
His further gait herein. In that the levies,
The lists, and full proportions are all made
Out of his subject: and we here dispatch
You good Cornelius, and you Voltemand,
For bearing of this greeting to old Norway,
Giving to you no further personal power
To business with the King, more than the scope
Of these dilated articles allow:
Farewell, and let your haste commend your duty.
VOLTEMAND: In that, and all things, will we show our
    duty.
KING: We doubt it nothing, heartily farewell.
      Exeunt Voltemand and Cornelius.
And now Laertes, what's the news with you?
You told us of some suit. What is't Laertes?
You cannot speak of reason to the Dane,
And lose your voice. What wouldst thou beg Laertes,
That shall not be my offer, not thy asking?

The head is not more native to the heart,
The hand more instrumental to the mouth,
Than is the throne of Denmark to thy father.
What wouldst thou have Laertes?
LAERTES: Dread my Lord,
Your leave and favour to return to France.
From whence, though willingly I came to Denmark
To show my duty in your Coronation,
Yet now I must confess, that duty done,
My thoughts and wishes bend again toward France,
And bow them to your gracious leave and pardon.
KING: Have you your father's leave? What says Polonius?
POLONIUS: He hath my Lord, [wrung from me my slow
    leave
By laboursome petition and at last
Upon his will I seal'd my hard consent;]
I do beseech you give him leave to go.
KING: Take thy fair hour Laertes, time be thine,
And thy best graces spend it at thy will:
But now my cousin Hamlet, and my son?
HAMLET: A little more than kin, and less than kind.
KING: How is it that the clouds still hang on you?
HAMLET: Not so my Lord, I am too much i' th' sun.
QUEEN: Good Hamlet cast thy nightly colour off,
And let thine eye look like a friend on Denmark.
Do not for ever with thy vailed lids
Seek for thy noble father in the dust;
Thou know'st 'tis common, all that lives must die,
Passing through nature, to eternity.
HAMLET: Ay Madam, it is common.
QUEEN: If it be,
Why seems it so particular with thee?
HAMLET: Seems Madam? nay, it is: I know not seems:

'Tis not alone my inky cloak, good mother,
Nor customary suits of solemn black,
Nor windy suspiration of forc'd breath.
No, nor the fruitful river in the eye,
Nor the dejected haviour of the visage,
Together with all forms, moods, shows of grief,
That can denote me truly. These indeed seem,
For they are actions that a man might play:
But I have that within, which passeth show;
These, but the trappings and the suits of woe.

KING: 'Tis sweet and commendable in your nature Hamlet,
To give these mourning duties to your father:
But you must know, your father lost a father,
That father lost, lost his, and the survivor bound
In filial obligation, for some term
To do obsequious sorrow. But to persever
In obstinate condolement, is a course
Of impious stubbornness. 'Tis unmanly grief,
It shows a will most incorrect to Heaven,
A heart unfortified, a mind impatient
An understanding simple, and unschool'd:
For, what we know must be, and is as common
As any the most vulgar thing to sense,
Why should we in our peevish opposition
Take it to heart? Fie, 'tis a fault to Heaven,
A fault against the dead, a fault to nature,
To reason most absurd, whose common theme
Is death of fathers, and who still hath cried,
From the first corse, till he that died to-day,
This must be so. We pray you throw to earth
This unprevailing woe, and think of us
As of a father; for let the world take note,
You are the most immediate to our Throne,

And with no less nobility of love,
Than that which dearest father bears his son,
Do I impart towards you. For your intent
In going back to school in Wittenberg,
It is most retrograde to our desire:
And we beseech you, bend you to remain
Here in the cheer and comfort of our eye,
Our chiefest courtier, cousin, and our son.

QUEEN: Let not thy mother lose her prayers Hamlet:
I prithee stay with us, go not to Wittenberg.

HAMLET: I shall in all my best obey you Madam.

KING: Why 'tis a loving, and a fair reply,
Be as ourself in Denmark. Madam come,
This gentle and unforc'd accord of Hamlet
Sits smiling to my heart; in grace whereof,
No jocund health that Denmark drinks to-day,
But the great cannon to the clouds shall tell,
And the King's rouse, the heavens shall bruit again,
Re-speaking earthly thunder. Come away.

Flourish. Exeunt all but Hamlet.

HAMLET: Oh, that this too too solid flesh, would melt,
Thaw, and resolve itself into a dew:
Or that the Everlasting had not fix'd
His canon 'gainst self-slaughter. O God, O God!
How weary, stale, flat and unprofitable
Seems to me all the uses of this world!
Fie on't! oh fie, fie, 'tis an unweeded garden
That grows to seed: things rank, and gross in nature
Possess it merely. That it should come to this:
But two months dead: nay, not so much; not two,
So excellent a King, that was to this
Hyperion to a satyr: so loving to my mother,
That he might not beteem the winds of heaven

Visit her face too roughly. Heaven and earth
Must I remember: why she would hang on him,
As if increase of appetite had grown
By what it fed on; and yet within a month!
Let me not think on't: Frailty, thy name is woman.
A little month, or ere those shoes were old,
With which she followed my poor father's body
Like Niobe, all tears. Why she, even she,
(O Heaven! A beast that wants discourse of reason
Would have mourn'd longer) married with mine uncle,
My father's brother: but no more like my father,
Than I to Hercules. Within a month!
Ere yet the salt of most unrighteous tears
Had left the flushing of her galled eyes,
She married. O most wicked speed, to post
With such dexterity to incestuous sheets:
It is not, nor it cannot come to good.
But break my heart, for I must hold my tongue.
            Enter Horatio, Barnardo, and Marcellus.
HORATIO: Hail to your Lordship.
HAMLET: I am glad to see you well:
    Horatio, or I do forget myself.
HORATIO: The same my Lord, and your poor servant ever.
HAMLET: Sir my good friend, I'll change that name with
    you:
    And what make you from Wittenberg Horatio?
    Marcellus.
MARCELLUS: My good Lord.
HAMLET: I am very glad to see you: good even sir.
    But what in faith make you from Wittenberg?
HORATIO: A truant disposition, good my Lord.
HAMLET: I would not have your enemy say so,
    Nor shall you do mine ear that violence,

To make it truster of your own report
Against yourself. I know you are no truant:
But what is your affair in Elsinore?
We'll teach you to drink deep, ere you depart.

HORATIO: My Lord, I came to see your father's funeral.

HAMLET: I pray thee do not mock me, fellow-student.
I think it was to see my mother's wedding.

HORATIO: Indeed my Lord, it followed hard upon.

HAMLET: Thrift, thrift, Horatio: the funeral baked-meats
Did coldly furnish forth the marriage tables;
Would I had met my dearest foe in heaven,
Or I had ever seen that day Horatio.
My father, methinks I see my father.

HORATIO: Oh where my Lord?

HAMLET: In my mind's eye, Horatio.

HORATIO: I saw him once; he was a goodly King.

HAMLET: He was a man, take him for all in all:
I shall not look upon his like again.

HORATIO: My Lord, I think I saw him yesternight.

HAMLET: Saw? who?

HORATIO: My Lord, the King your father.

HAMLET: The King my father?

HORATIO: Season your admiration for a while
With an attent ear; till I may deliver
Upon the witness of these gentlemen,
This marvel to you.

HAMLET: For God's love let me hear.

HORATIO: Two nights together, had these gentlemen
(Marcellus and Barnardo) on their watch
In the dead waste and middle of the night
Been thus encounter'd. A figure like your father,
Arm'd at all points exactly, cap-a-pe,
Appears before them, and with solemn march

Goes slow and stately: by them thrice he walk'd,
By their oppress'd and fear-surprised eyes,
Within his truncheon's length; whilst they, distill'd
Almost to jelly with the act of fear,
Stand dumb and speak not to him. This to me
In dreadful secrecy impart they did,
And I with them the third night kept the watch,
Whereas they had deliver'd both in time,
Form of the thing, each word made true and good,
The apparition comes. I knew your father:
These hands are not more like.

HAMLET: But where was this?

MARCELLUS: My Lord upon the platform where we
watch'd.

HAMLET: Did you not speak to it?

HORATIO: My Lord, I did;
But answer made it none: yet once methought
It lifted up its head, and did address
Itself to motion, like as it would speak:
But even then, the morning cock crew loud;
And at the sound it shrunk in haste away,
And vanish'd from our sight.

HAMLET: 'Tis very strange.

HORATIO: As I do live my honour'd Lord 'tis true;
And we did think it writ down in our duty
To let you know of it.

HAMLET: Indeed, indeed sirs; but this troubles me.
Hold you the watch to-night?

BOTH: We do my Lord.

HAMLET: Arm'd, say you?

BOTH: Arm'd, my Lord.

HAMLET: From top to toe?

BOTH: My Lord, from head to foot.

HAMLET: Then saw you not his face?

HORATIO: O yes, my Lord, he wore his beaver up.

HAMLET: What, look'd he frowningly?

HORATIO: A countenance more in sorrow than in anger.

HAMLET: Pale, or red?

HORATIO: Nay, very pale.

HAMLET: And fix'd his eyes upon you?

HORATIO: Most constantly.

HAMLET: I would I had been there.

HORATIO: It would have much amaz'd you.

HAMLET: Very like, very like: stay'd it long?

HORATIO: While one with moderate haste might tell a
    hundred.

BOTH: Longer, longer.

HORATIO: Not when I saw't.

HAMLET: His beard was grizzled, no?

HORATIO: It was, as I have seen it in his life,
    A sable silver'd.

HAMLET: I will watch to-night;
    Perchance 'twill walk again.

HORATIO: I warrant you it will.

HAMLET: If it assume my noble father's person,
    I'll speak to it, though Hell itself should gape
    And bid me hold my peace. I pray you all,
    If you have hitherto conceal'd this sight;
    Let it be tenable in your silence still:
    And whatsoever else shall hap to-night,
    Give it an understanding but no tongue;
    I will requite your loves; so, fare you well:
    Upon the platform 'twixt eleven and twelve,
    I'll visit you.

ALL: Our duty to your Honour.
                    Exeunt.

HAMLET: Your love, as mine to you: farewell.
My father's spirit in arms? all is not well:
I doubt some foul play; would the night were come;
Till then sit still my soul; foul deeds will rise,
Though all the earth o'erwhelm them to men's eyes.

Exit.

I. 3

Enter Laertes and Ophelia.

LAERTES: My necessaries are embark'd; farewell:
And sister, as the winds give benefit,
And convoy is assistant, do not sleep,
But let me hear from you.

OPHELIA: Do you doubt that?

LAERTES: For Hamlet, and the trifling of his favours,
Hold it a fashion and a toy in blood:
A violet in the youth of primy nature;
Froward, not permanent; sweet not lasting,
The perfume and suppliance of a minute,
No more.

OPHELIA: No more but so?

LAERTES: Think it no more:
For nature crescent does not grow alone,
In thews and bulk: but as this temple waxes,
The inward service of the mind and soul
Grows wide withal. Perhaps he loves you now,
And now no soil nor cautel doth besmirch
The virtue of his will: but you must fear,
His greatness weigh'd, his will is not his own;
For he himself is subject to his birth:
He may not, as unvalued persons do,
Carve for himself; for, on his choice depends

The sanctity and health of this whole State,
And therefore must his choice be circumscrib'd
Unto the voice and yielding of that body,
Whereof he is the head. Then if he says he loves you,
It fits your wisdom so far to believe it,
As he in his particular act and place
May give his saying deed: which is no further,
Than the main voice of Denmark goes withal.
Then weigh what loss your honour may sustain,
If with too credent ear you list his songs;
Or lose your heart; or your chaste treasure open
To his unmaster'd importunity.
Fear it Ophelia, fear it my dear sister,
And keep within the rear of your affection,
Out of the shot and danger of desire.
The chariest maid is prodigal enough,
If she unmask her beauty to the Moon:
Virtue itself 'scapes not calumnious strokes,
The canker galls the infants of the spring
Too oft before their buttons be disclos'd,
And in the morn and liquid dew of youth,
Contagious blastments are most imminent.
Be wary then, best safety lies in fear;
Youth to itself rebels, though none else near.
OPHELIA: I shall th' effect of this good lesson keep,
As watchman to my heart: but good my brother,
Do not as some ungracious pastors do,
Show me the steep and thorny way to heaven,
Whiles like a puff'd and reckless libertine
Himself, the primrose path of dalliance treads,
And wreaks not his own rede.
LAERTES: Oh, fear me not.
Enter Polonius.

I stay too long; but here my father comes:
A double blessing is a double grace;
Occasion smiles upon a second leave.
POLONIUS: Yet here Laertes? Aboard, aboard for shame,
The wind sits in the shoulder of your sail,
And you are stay'd for; there, my blessing with thee;
And these few precepts in thy memory,
See thou character. Give thy thoughts no tongue,
Nor any unproportion'd thought his act:
Be thou familiar; but by no means vulgar:
The friends thou hast, and their adoption tried,
Grapple them to thy soul, with hoops of steel:
But do not dull thy palm, with entertainment
Of each unhatch'd, unfledg'd, comrade. Beware
Of entrance to a quarrel: but being in
Bear't that th' opposed may beware of thee.
Give every man thine ear; but few thy voice:
Take each man's censure; but reserve thy judgment:
Costly thy habit as thy purse can buy;
But not express'd in fancy; rich, not gaudy:
For the apparel oft proclaims the man,
And they in France of the best rank and station,
Or of a most select and generous, chief in that.
Neither a borrower, nor a lender be;
For loan oft loses both itself and friend:
And borrowing dulls the edge of husbandry.
This above all; to thine ownself be true:
And it must follow, as the night the day,
Thou canst not then be false to any man.
Farewell: my blessing season this in thee.
LAERTES: Most humbly do I take my leave, my Lord.
POLONIUS: The time invites you, go, your servants tend.
LAERTES: Farewell Ophelia, and remember well

  What I have said to you.

OPHELIA: 'Tis in my memory lock'd,
  And you yourself shall keep the key of it.

LAERTES: Farewell.

Exit Laertes.

POLONIUS: What is't Ophelia he hath said to you?

OPHELIA: So please you, something touching the Lord
  Hamlet.

POLONIUS: Marry, well bethought:
  'Tis told me he hath very oft of late
  Given private time to you: and you yourself
  Have of your audience been most free and bounteous.
  If it be so, as so 'tis put on me;
  And that in way of caution: I must tell you,
  You do not understand yourself so clearly,
  As it behoves my daughter, and your honour.
  What is between you, give me up the truth.

OPHELIA: He hath my Lord of late, made many tenders
  Of his affection for me.

POLONIUS: Affection, pooh. You speak like a green girl,
  Unsifted in such perilous circumstance.
  Do you believe his tenders, as you call them?

OPHELIA: I do not know, my Lord, what I should think.

POLONIUS: Marry I'll teach you; think yourself a baby,
  That you have ta'en his tenders for true pay,
  Which are not sterling. Tender yourself more dearly;
  Or not to crack the wind of the poor phrase,
  Roaming it thus, you'll tender me a fool.

OPHELIA: My Lord, he hath importun'd me with love,
  In honourable fashion.

POLONIUS: Ay, fashion you may call it, go to, go to.

OPHELIA: And hath given countenance to his speech, my
  Lord,

With all the vows of Heaven.

POLONIUS: Ay, springes to catch woodcocks. I do know
When the blood burns, how prodigal the soul
Lends the tongue vows: these blazes, daughter,
Giving more light than heat, extinct in both,
Even in their promise, as it is a-making,
You must not take for fire. From this time
Be something scanter of your maiden presence;
Set your entreatments at a higher rate,
Than a command to parley. For Lord Hamlet,
Believe so much in him, that he is young,
And with a larger tether may he walk,
Than may be given you. In few, Ophelia,
Do not believe his vows; for they are brokers,
Not of that dye which their investments show,
But mere implorators of unholy suits,
Breathing like sanctified and pious bawds,
The better to beguile. This is for all:
I would not, in plain terms, from this time forth,
Have you so slander any moment leisure,
As to give words or talk with the Lord Hamlet:
Look to 't, I charge you; come your ways.

OPHELIA: I shall obey my Lord.

Exeunt.

I. 4

Enter Hamlet, Horatio, and Marcellus.

HAMLET: The air bites shrewdly: it is very cold.

HORATIO: It is a nipping and an eager air.

HAMLET: What hour now?

HORATIO: I think it lacks of twelve.

MARCELLUS: No, it is struck.

HORATIO: Indeed I heard it not: then it draws near the
  season,
Wherein the spirit held his wont to walk.
      A flourish of trumpets, and two pieces go off.
What does this mean my Lord?
HAMLET: The King doth wake to-night, and takes his
  rouse,
Keeps wassail, and the swaggering up-spring reels:
And as he drains his draughts of Rhenish down,
The kettle-drum and trumpet thus bray out
The triumph of his pledge.
HORATIO: Is it a custom?
HAMLET: Ay marry is't;
But to my mind, though I am native here,
And to the manner born, it is a custom
More honour'd in the breach, than the observance.
[This heavy-headed revel east and west
Makes us traduc'd, and tax'd of other nations:
They clepe us drunkards, and with swinish phrase
Soil our addition; and indeed it takes
From our achievements, though perform'd at height,
The pith and marrow of our attribute:
So oft it chances in particular men,
That for some vicious mole of nature in them,
As in their birth wherein they are not guilty,
(Since nature cannot choose his origin)
By their o'ergrowth of some complexion
Oft breaking down the pales and forts of reason,
Or by some habit, that too much o'er-leavens
The form of plausive manners, that these men,
Carrying I say the stamp of one defect,
Being nature's livery, or fortune's star,
Their virtues else be they as pure as grace,

As infinite as man may undergo,
Shall in the general censure take corruption
From that particular fault: the dram of eale
Doth all the noble substance of a doubt
To his own scandal.]

Enter Ghost.

HORATIO: Look my Lord, it comes.
HAMLET: Angels and ministers of grace defend us:
Be thou a spirit of health, or goblin damn'd,
Bring with thee airs from Heaven, or blasts from Hell,
Be thy intents wicked or charitable,
Thou com'st in such a questionable shape
That I will speak to thee. I'll call thee Hamlet,
King, father, royal Dane: Oh, answer me,
Let me not burst in ignorance; but tell
Why thy canoniz'd bones hearsed in death,
Have burst their cerements, why the sepulchre
Wherein we saw thee quietly inurn'd,
Hath op'd his ponderous and marble jaws,
To cast thee up again? What may this mean?
That thou dead corse again in complete steel,
Revisit'st thus the glimpses of the Moon,
Making night hideous? and we fools of nature,
So horridly to shake our disposition,
With thoughts beyond the reaches of our souls;
Say, why is this? wherefore? what should we do?

Ghost beckons Hamlet.

HORATIO: It beckons you to go away with it,
As if it some impartment did desire
To you alone.
MARCELLUS: Look with what courteous action
It wafts you to a more removed ground:
But do not go with it.

HORATIO: No, by no means.

HAMLET: It will not speak: then I will follow it.

HORATIO: Do not my Lord.

HAMLET: Why, what should be the fear?
  I do not set my life at a pin's fee;
  And for my soul, what can it do to that,
  Being a thing immortal as itself:
  It waves me forth again; I'll follow it.

HORATIO: What if it tempt you toward the flood my
    Lord?
  Or to the dreadful summit of the cliff,
  That beetles o'er his base into the sea,
  And there assume some other horrible form,
  Which might deprive your sovereignty of reason,
  And draw you into madness? think of it:
  [The very place puts toys of desperation
  Without more motive, into every brain
  That looks so many fathoms to the sea
  And hears it roar beneath.]

HAMLET: It wafts me still:
  Go on, I'll follow thee.

MARCELLUS: You shall not go my Lord.

HAMLET: Hold off your hands.

HORATIO: Be rul'd, you shall not go.

HAMLET: My fate cries out,
  And makes each petty arter in this body
  As hardy as the Nemean lion's nerve:
  Still am I call'd? Unhand me gentlemen:
  By Heaven, I'll make a ghost of him that lets me:
  I say away, go on, I'll follow thee.
              Exeunt Ghost and Hamlet.

HORATIO: He waxes desperate with imagination.

MARCELLUS: Let's follow; 'tis not fit thus to obey him.

HORATIO: Have after, to what issue will this come?

MARCELLUS: Something is rotten in the state of Denmark.

HORATIO: Heaven will direct it.

MARCELLUS: Nay, let's follow him.

Exeunt.

I. 5

Enter Ghost and Hamlet.

HAMLET: Where wilt thou lead me? speak; I'll go no further.

GHOST: Mark me.

HAMLET: I will.

GHOST: My hour is almost come,
When I to sulphurous and tormenting flames
Must render up myself.

HAMLET: Alas poor ghost.

GHOST: Pity me not, but lend thy serious hearing
To what I shall unfold.

HAMLET: Speak, I am bound to hear.

GHOST: So art thou to revenge, when thou shalt hear.

HAMLET: What?

GHOST: I am thy father's spirit,
Doom'd for a certain term to walk the night;
And for the day confin'd to fast in fires,
Till the foul crimes done in my days of nature
Are burnt and purg'd away. But that I am forbid
To tell the secrets of my prison-house,
I could a tale unfold, whose lightest word
Would harrow up thy soul, freeze thy young blood,
Make thy two eyes like stars, start from their spheres,
Thy knotty and combined locks to part,

And each particular hair to stand an end,
Like quills upon the fretful porpentine:
But this eternal blazon must not be
To ears of flesh and blood; list, Hamlet, oh list.
If thou didst ever thy dear father love.

HAMLET: O God!

GHOST: Revenge his foul and most unnatural murther.

HAMLET: Murther?

GHOST: Murther most foul, as in the best it is;
But this most foul, strange, and unnatural.

HAMLET: Haste, haste me to know it,
   that I with wings as swift
As meditation, or the thoughts of love,
May sweep to my revenge.

GHOST: I find thee apt,
And duller shouldst thou be than the fat weed
That roots itself in ease on Lethe wharf,
Wouldn't thou not stir in this. Now Hamlet hear:
It's given out, that sleeping in my orchard,
A serpent stung me: so the whole ear of Denmark,
Is by a forged process of my death
Rankly abus'd: but know thou noble youth,
The serpent that did sting thy father's life,
Now wears his crown.

HAMLET: O my prophetic soul,
Mine uncle?

GHOST: Ay that incestuous, that adulterate beast
With witchcraft of his wits, with traitorous gifts
(O wicked wit, and gifts, that have the power
So to seduce!) won to his shameful lust
The will of my most seeming-virtuous Queen:
O Hamlet, what a falling-off was there,
From me, whose love was of that dignity,

That it went hand in hand, even with the vow
I made to her in marriage; and to decline
Upon a wretch whose natural gifts were poor
To those of mine.
But virtue, as it never will be moved,
Though lewdness court it in a shape of Heaven,
So lust, though to a radiant angel link'd,
Will sate itself in a celestial bed,
And prey on garbage.
But soft, methinks I scent the morning's air;
Brief let me be: sleeping within my orchard,
My custom always in the afternoon,
Upon my secure hour thy uncle stole
With juice of cursed hebonon in a vial,
And in the porches of mine ears did pour
The leperous distilment; whose effect
Holds such an enmity with blood of man,
That swift as quicksilver it courses through
The natural gates and alleys of the body;
And with a sudden vigour it doth posset
And curd, like eager droppings into milk,
The thin and wholesome blood: so did it mine;
And a most instant tetter bak'd about,
Most lazar-like, with vile and loathsome crust,
All my smooth body.
Thus was I, sleeping, by a brother's hand,
Of life, of crown, and Queen, at once dispatch'd;
Cut off even in the blossoms of my sin,
Unhousel'd, disappointed, unaneled.
No reckoning made, but sent to my account
With all my imperfections on my head;
O horrible, O horrible, most horrible;
If thou hast nature in thee bear it not;

Let not the royal bed of Denmark be
A couch for luxury and damned incest.
But howsoever thou pursuest this act,
Taint not thy mind; nor let thy soul contrive
Against thy mother aught; leave her to heaven,
And to those thorns that in her bosom lodge,
To prick and sting her. Fare thee well at once;
The glow-worm shows the matin to be near,
And 'gins to pale his uneffectual fire:
Adieu, adieu, Hamlet: remember me.
                        Exit.
HAMLET: Oh all you host of Heaven! Oh Earth: what
    else?
And shall I couple Hell? Oh fie: hold my heart;
And you my sinews grow not instant old;
But bear me stiffly up: remember thee?
Ay thou poor ghost, while memory holds a seat
In this distracted globe: remember thee?
Yea, from the table of my memory,
I'll wipe away all trivial fond records,
All saws of books, all forms, all pressures past,
That youth and observation copied there;
And thy commandment all alone shall live
Within the book and volume of my brain,
Unmix'd with baser matter; yes, yes, by Heaven:
O most pernicious woman!
Oh villain, villain, smiling damned villain!
My tables, my tables; meet it is I set it down,
That one may smile, and smile and be a villain;
At least I'm sure it may be so in Denmark;
So uncle there you are: now to my word;
It is; Adieu, adieu, remember me;
I have sworn't.

MARCELLUS:
HORATIO: } *Within.* My Lord, my Lord.

Enter Horatio and Marcellus.

MARCELLUS: Lord Hamlet.

HORATIO: Heaven secure him.

HAMLET: So be it.

HORATIO: Illo, ho, ho, my Lord.

HAMLET: Hillo, ho, ho, boy; come bird, come.

MARCELLUS: How is't my noble Lord?

HORATIO: What news, my Lord?

HAMLET: O wonderful!

HORATIO: Good my Lord tell it.

HAMLET: No you will reveal it.

HORATIO: Not I, my Lord, by Heaven.

MARCELLUS: Nor I, my Lord.

HAMLET: How say you then, would heart of man once
    think it?
  But you'll be secret?

BOTH: Ay, by Heaven, my Lord.

HAMLET: There's ne'er a villain dwelling in all Denmark
  But he's an arrant knave.

HORATIO: There needs no ghost my Lord, come from the
    grave,
  To tell us this.

HAMLET: Why right, you are i' th' right;
  And so, without more circumstance at all,
  I hold it fit that we shake hands, and part;
  You, as your business and desire shall point you:
  For every man hath business and desire,
  Such as it is: and for my own part,
  Look you, I'll go pray.

HORATIO: These are but wild and whirling words my
    Lord.

HAMLET: I'm sorry they offend you, heartily:
  Yes faith, heartily.

HORATIO: There's no offence my Lord.

HAMLET: Yes, by Saint Patrick, but there is, Horatio,
  And much offence too, touching this vision here:
  It is an honest ghost, that let me tell you:
  For your desire to know what is between us,
  O'ermaster't as you may. And now good friends,
  As you are friends, scholars and soldiers,
  Give me one poor request.

HORATIO: What is't my Lord? we will.

HAMLET: Never make known what you have seen to-
  night.

BOTH: My Lord, we will not.

HAMLET: Nay, but swear't.

HORATIO: In faith my Lord, not I.

MARCELLUS: Nor I my Lord: in faith.

HAMLET: Upon my sword.

MARCELLUS: We have sworn my Lord already.

HAMLET: Indeed, upon my sword, indeed.

        Ghost cries under the stage.

GHOST: Swear.

HAMLET: Ah ha boy say'st thou so? art thou there,
  truepenny?
  Come on, you hear this fellow in the cellarage,
  Consent to swear.

HORATIO: Propose the oath my Lord.

HAMLET: Never to speak of this that you have seen.
  Swear by my sword.

GHOST: Swear.

HAMLET: *Hic et ubique?* Then we'll shift our ground.
  Come hither gentlemen,
  And lay your hands again upon my sword,

Never to speak of this that you have heard:
Swear by my sword.

GHOST: Swear.

HAMLET: Well said old mole, canst work i' th' ground so
fast?
A worthy pioner, once more remove good friends.

HORATIO: O day and night: but this is wondrous
strange.

HAMLET: And therefore as a stranger give it welcome.
There are more things in Heaven and Earth, Horatio,
Than are dreamt of in our philosophy.
But come,
Here as before, never so help you mercy,
How strange or odd soe'er I bear myself;
(As I perchance hereafter shall think meet
To put an antic disposition on:
That you at such times seeing me, never shall
With arms encumber'd thus, or thus, head-shake;
Or by pronouncing of some doubtful phrase;
As well, we know, or we could and if we would,
Or if we list to speak, or There be and if there might,
Or such ambiguous giving out to note,
That you know aught of me; this not to do:
So grace and mercy at your most need help you:
Swear.

GHOST: Swear.

HAMLET: Rest, rest perturbed spirit: so gentlemen,
With all my love I do commend me to you;
And what so poor a man as Hamlet is,
May do t' express his love and friending to you,
God willing shall not lack: let us go in together,
And still your fingers on your lips I pray.
The time is out of joint: O cursed spite,

That ever I was born to set it right.
Nay, come let's go together.
Exeunt.

II.1

Enter Polonius, and Reynaldo.

POLONIUS: Give him this money, and these notes Reynaldo.

REYNALDO: I will my Lord.

POLONIUS: You shall do marvellous wisely, good Reynaldo.
Before you visit him, to make inquire
Of his behaviour.

REYNALDO: My Lord, I did intend it.

POLONIUS: Marry, well said; very well said. Look you sir,
Inquire me first what Danskers are in Paris;
And how, and who: what means; and where they keep:
What company, at what expense: and finding
By this encompassment and drift of question,
That they do know my son, come you more nearer
Than your particular demands will touch it,
Take you as 'twere some distant knowledge of him,
As thus, I know his father and his friends,
And in part him. Do you mark this Reynaldo?

REYNALDO: Ay, very well my Lord.

POLONIUS: And in part him, but you may say, not well;
But if't be he I mean, he's very wild;
Addicted so and so; and there put on him
What forgeries you please: marry, none so rank,
As may dishonour him; take heed of that:
But sir, such wanton, wild, and usual slips,

As are companions noted and most known
To youth and liberty.

REYNALDO: As gaming my Lord.

POLONIUS: Ay, or drinking, fencing, swearing, quarrell-
ing, drabbing.

You may go so far.

REYNALDO: My Lord that would dishonour him.

POLONIUS: Faith no, as you may season it in the charge;
You must not put another scandal on him,
That he is open to incontinency;
That's not my meaning: but breathe his faults so quaintly,
That they may seem the taints of liberty;
The flash and outbreak of a fiery mind,
A savageness in unreclaimed blood
Of general assault.

REYNALDO: But my good Lord –

POLONIUS: Wherefore should you do this?

REYNALDO: Ay my Lord,
I would know that.

POLONIUS: Marry sir, here's my drift,
And I believe it is a fetch of warrant:
You laying these slight sullies on my son,
As 'twere a thing a little soil'd i' th' working:
Mark you,
Your party in converse, him you would sound,
Having ever seen in the prenominate crimes,
The youth you breathe of guilty, be assur'd
He closes with you in this consequence:
Good sir, or so, or friend, or gentleman,
According to the phrase and the addition,
Of man and country.

REYNALDO: Very good my Lord.

POLONIUS: And then sir does he this, he does: what was I

about to say? By the mass I was about to say something:
where did I leave?

REYNALDO: At closes in the consequence: at friend, or so,
and gentleman.

POLONIUS: At closes in the consequence, at marry,
He closes with you thus. I know the gentleman,
I saw him yesterday, or t'other day;
Or then, or then with such and such; and as you say,
There was a' gaming, there o'ertook in 's rouse,
There falling out at tennis; or perchance,
I saw him enter such a house of sale;
Videlicet, a brothel, or so forth.
See you now;
Your bait of falsehood, takes this carp of truth;
And thus do we of wisdom and of reach
With windlasses, and with assays of bias,
By indirections find directions out:
So by my former lecture and advice
Shall you my son; you have me, have you not?

REYNALDO: My Lord, I have.

POLONIUS: God buy you; fare you well.

REYNALDO: Good my Lord.

POLONIUS: Observe his inclination in yourself.

REYNALDO: I shall my Lord.

POLONIUS: And let him ply his music.

REYNALDO: Well, my Lord.

Exit.

POLONIUS: Farewell:

Enter Ophelia.

How now Ophelia, what's the matter?

OPHELIA: Alas my Lord, I have been so affrighted.

POLONIUS: With what, in the name of Heaven?

OPHELIA: My Lord, as I was sewing in my chamber,

Lord Hamlet with his doublet all unbrac'd,
No hat upon his head, his stockings foul'd,
Ungarter'd, and down-gyved to his ankle,
Pale as his shirt, his knees knocking each other,
And with a look so piteous in purport,
As if he had been loosed out of hell,
To speak of horrors: he comes before me.

POLONIUS: Mad for thy love?

OPHELIA: My Lord, I do not know:
But truly I do fear it.

POLONIUS: What said he?

OPHELIA: He took me by the wrist, and held me hard;
Then goes he to the length of all his arm;
And with his other hand thus o'er his brow,
He falls to such perusal of my face
As he would draw it. Long stay'd he so;
At last, a little shaking of mine arm:
And thrice his head thus waving up and down;
He rais'd a sigh, so piteous and profound,
As it did seem to shatter all his bulk,
And end his being. That done, he lets me go,
And with his head over his shoulder turn'd,
He seem'd to find his way without his eyes,
For out a doors he went without their help;
And to the last bended their light on me.

POLONIUS: Come, go with me, I will go seek the King;
This is the very ecstasy of love,
Whose violent property fordoes itself,
And leads the will to desperate undertakings,
As oft as any passion under Heaven,
That does afflict our natures. I am sorry,
What, have you given him any hard words of late?

OPHELIA: No my good Lord: but as you did command,

I did repel his letters, and denied
His access to me.
POLONIUS: That hath made him mad.
I am sorry that with better heed and judgement
I had not quoted him. I fear'd he did but trifle,
And meant to wrack thee: but beshrew my jealousy:
It seems it is as proper to our age,
To cast beyond ourselves in our opinions,
As it is common for the younger sort
To lack discretion. Come, go we to the King,
This must be known, which being kept close might
  move
More grief to hide, than hate to utter love.
Come.

Exeunt.

II. 2

Flourish.
Enter King and Queen, Rosencrantz and Guildenstern,
with others.
KING: Welcome dear Rosencrantz and Guildenstern.
Moreover, that we much did long to see you,
The need we have to use you, did provoke
Our hasty sending. Something have you heard
Of Hamlet's transformation: so I call it,
Sith nor th' exterior nor the inward man
Resembles that it was. What should it be
More than his father's death, that thus hath put him
So much from th' understanding of himself,
I cannot deem of: I entreat you both,
That being of so young days brought up with him:
And sith so neighbour'd to his youth, and humour,

That you vouchsafe your rest here in our Court
Some little time: so by your companies
To draw him on to pleasures, and to gather
So much as from occasions you may glean,
[Whether aught to us unknown afflicts him thus]
That open'd lies within our remedy.

QUEEN: Good gentlemen, he hath much talk'd of you,
And sure I am, two men there are not living,
To whom he more adheres. If it will please you
To show us so much gentry, and good will,
As to expend your time with us awhile,
For the supply and profit of our hope,
Your visitation shall receive such thanks
As fits a King's remembrance.

ROSENCRANTZ: Both your Majesties
Might by the sovereign power you have of us,
Put your dread pleasures, more into command
Than to entreaty.

GUILDENSTERN: We both obey,
And here give up ourselves, in the full bent,
To lay our services freely at your feet,
To be commanded.

KING: Thanks Rosencrantz, and gentle Guildenstern.

QUEEN: Thanks Guildernstern and gentle Rosencrantz.
And I beseech you instantly to visit
My too much changed son. Go some of ye,
And bring the gentlemen where Hamlet is.

GUILDENSTERN: Heavens make our presence and our
    practices
Pleasant and helpful to him.

Exeunt with others.

QUEEN: Ay, amen.

Enter Polonius.

POLONIUS: Th' ambassadors from Norway, my good Lord,
Are joyfully return'd.

KING: Thou still hast been the father of good news.

POLONIUS: Have I, my Lord? I assure you, my good Liege,
I hold my duty, as I hold my soul,
Both to my God, and to my gracious King:
And I do think, or else this brain of mine
Hunts not the trail of policy, so sure
As it hath used to do, that I have found
The very cause of Hamlet's lunacy.

KING: O speak of that, that do I long to hear.

POLONIUS: Give first admittance to th' ambassadors,
My news shall be the fruit to that great feast.

KING: Thyself do grace to them, and bring them in.

Exit Polonius.

He tells me my sweet Queen, that he hath found
The head and source of all your son's distemper.

QUEEN: I doubt it is no other, but the main,
His father death, and our o'erhasty marriage.

Enter Polonius, Voltemand and Cornelius.

KING: Well, we shall sift him.
Welcome my good friends:
Say Voltemand, what from our brother Norway?

VOLTEMAND: Most fair return of greetings, and desires.
Upon our first, he sent us to suppress
His nephew's levies, which to him appear'd
To be a preparation 'gainst the Polack;
But better look'd into, he truly found
It was against your Highness, whereat grieved,
That so his sickness, age, and impotence
Was falsely borne in hand, sends out arrests
On Fortinbras, which he (in brief) obeys,

Receives rebuke from Norway: and in fine,
Makes vow before his uncle, never more
To give th' assay of arms against your Majesty.
Whereon old Norway, overcome with joy,
Gives him three thousand crowns in annual fee,
And his commission to employ those soldiers
So levied as before, against the Polack:
With an entreaty herein further shown,
That it might please you to give quiet pass
Through your dominions, for his enterprise,
On such regards of safety and allowance,
As therein are set down.

KING: It likes us well:
And at our more consider'd time we'll read,
Answer, and think upon this business.
Meantime we thank you, for your well-took labour.
Go to your rest, at night we'll feast together.
Most welcome home.

Exeunt Ambassadors.

POLONIUS: This business is very well ended.
My Liege, and Madam, to expostulate
What Majesty should be, what duty is,
Why day is day; night, night; and time is time,
Were nothing but to waste night, day, and time.
Therefore, since brevity is the soul of wit,
And tediousness, the limbs and outward flourishes,
I will be brief. Your noble son is mad:
Mad I call it; for to define true madness,
What is't, but to be nothing else but mad.
But let that go.

QUEEN: More matter, with less art.

POLONIUS: Madam, I swear I use no art at all:
That he is mad, 'tis true: 'tis true 'tis pity,

And pity it is true: a foolish figure,
But farewell it: for I will use no art.
Mad let us grant him then: and now remains
That we find out the cause of this effect,
Or rather say, the cause of this defect;
For this effect defective, comes by cause:
Thus it remains, and the remainder thus.
Perpend,
I have a daughter: have, while she is mine,
Who in her duty and obedience, mark,
Hath given me this: now gather, and surmise.

The Letter.

*To the Celestial, and my Soul's idol, the most beautified
   Ophelia.*

That's an ill phrase, a vile phrase, beautified is a vile
   phrase: but you shall hear:

These in her excellent white bosom, these &c.

QUEEN: Came this from Hamlet to her?

POLONIUS: Good Madam stay awhile, I will be faithful.

> *Doubt thou, the Stars are fire,*
> *Doubt that the Sun doth move,*
> *Doubt Truth to be a liar,*
> *But never doubt, I love.*

*O dear Ophelia, I am ill at these numbers: I have not Art
   to reckon my groans; but that I love thee best, O most
   Best, believe it. Adieu.*

> *Thine evermore most dear Lady,*
> *whilst this machine is to him,*
>
> HAMLET.

This in obedience hath my daughter show'd me:
And more above hath his solicitings,
As they fell out by time, by means, and place,
All given to mine ear.

KING: But how hath she receiv'd his love?

POLONIUS: What do you think of me?

KING: As of a man, faithful and honourable.

POLONIUS: I would fain prove so. But what might you
    think?
  When I had seen this hot love on the wing,
  As I perceived it, I must tell you that
  Before my daughter told me, what might you,
  Or my dear Majesty your Queen here, think,
  If I had play'd the desk or table-book,
  Or given my heart a winking, mute and dumb,
  Or look'd upon this love, with idle sight,
  What might you think? No, I went round to work,
  And my young mistress thus I did bespeak,
  Lord Hamlet is a Prince out of thy star,
  This must not be: and then, I precepts gave her,
  That she should lock herself from his resort,
  Admit no messengers, receive no tokens:
  Which done, she took the fruits of my advice,
  And he repulsed, a short tale to make,
  Fell into a sadness, then into a fast,
  Thence to a watch, thence into a weakness,
  Thence to a lightness, and by this declension
  Into the madness wherein now he raves,
  And all we wail for.

KING: Do you think 'tis this?

QUEEN: It may be very likely.

POLONIUS: Hath there been such a time. I'ld fain know
    that,
  That I have positively said, 'Tis so,
  When it prov'd otherwise?

KING: Not that I know.

POLONIUS: Take this from this, if this be otherwise;

If circumstances lead me, I will find
Where truth is hid, though it were hid indeed
Within the Centre.

KING: How may we try it further?

POLONIUS: You know sometimes he walks four hours together,
Here in the lobby.

QUEEN: So he does indeed.

POLONIUS: At such a time I'll loose my daughter to him;
Be you and I behind an arras then;
Mark the encounter: if he love her not,
And be not from his reason fall'n thereon;
Let me be no assistant for a state,
But keep a farm and carters.

KING: We will try it.

Enter Hamlet, reading on a book.

QUEEN: But look where sadly the poor wretch comes reading.

POLONIUS: Away I do beseech you, both away,
I'll board him presently.

Exeunt King and Queen.

O give me leave.
How does my good Lord Hamlet?

HAMLET: Well, God-a-mercy.

POLONIUS: Do you know me, my Lord?

HAMLET: Excellent, excellent well: you are a fishmonger.

POLONIUS: Not I my Lord.

HAMLET: Then I would you were so honest a man.

POLONIUS: Honest, my Lord?

HAMLET: Ay sir, to be honest as this world goes, is to be one man pick'd out of two thousand.

POLONIUS: That's very true, my Lord.

HAMLET: For if the Sun breed maggots in a dead dog, being a good kissing carrion – Have you a daughter?

POLONIUS: I have my Lord.

HAMLET: Let her not walk i' th' Sun: conception is a blessing, but not as your daughter may conceive. Friend look to't.

POLONIUS: How say you by that? Still harping on my daughter: yet he knew me not at first; he said I was a fishmonger: he is far gone, far gone, and truly in my youth, I suffered much extremity for love: very near this. I'll speak to him again. What do you read my Lord?

HAMLET: Words, words, words.

POLONIUS: What is the matter, my Lord?

HAMLET: Between who?

POLONIUS: I mean the matter that you read, my Lord.

HAMLET: Slanders sir: for the satirical slave says here, that old men have grey beards; that their faces are wrinkled; their eyes purging thick amber, or plum-tree gum: and that they have a plentiful lack of wit, together with weak hams. All which sir, though I most powerfully, and potently believe; yet I hold it not honesty to have it thus set down: for yourself sir, should be old as I am, if like a crab you could go backward.

POLONIUS: Though this be madness, yet there is method in't: will you walk out of the air my Lord?

HAMLET: Into my grave?

POLONIUS: Indeed that is out o' th 'air: how pregnant (sometimes) his replies are! a happiness, that often madness hits on, which reason and sanity could not so prosperously be deliver'd of. I will leave him, and suddenly contrive the means of meeting between him, and my daughter. My honourable Lord, I will most humbly take my leave of you.

HAMLET: You cannot sir take from me any thing, that I will more willingly part withal, except my life, my life.

POLONIUS: Fare you well my Lord.

HAMLET: These tedious old fools.

Enter Rosencrantz and Guildenstern.

POLONIUS: You go to seek my Lord Hamlet; there he is.

ROSENCRANTZ: God save you sir.

Exit Polonius.

GUILDENSTERN: My honour'd Lord!

ROSENCRANTZ: My most dear Lord!

HAMLET: My excellent good friends! How dost thou Guildenstern? Ah Rosencrantz; good lads: how do ye both?

ROSENCRANTZ: As the indifferent children of the earth.

GUILDENSTERN: Happy, in that we are not over-happy: On Fortune's cap, we are not the very button.

HAMLET: Nor the soles of her shoe?

ROSENCRANTZ: Neither my Lord.

HAMLET: Then you live about her waist, or in the middle of her favour?

GUILDENSTERN: Faith, her privates, we.

HAMLET: In the secret parts of Fortune? Oh, most true: she is a strumpet. What's the news?

ROSENCRANTZ: None my Lord; but that the world's grown honest.

HAMLET: Then is Doomsday near: but your news is not true. Let me question more in particular: what have you my good friends, deserved at the hands of Fortune, that she sends you to prison hither?

GUILDENSTERN: Prison, my Lord?

HAMLET: Denmark's a prison.

ROSENCRANTZ: Then is the world one.

HAMLET: A goodly one, in which there are many confines, wards, and dungeons; Denmark being one o' th' worst.

ROSENCRANTZ: We think not so my Lord.

HAMLET: Why then 'tis none to you; for there is nothing either good or bad, but thinking makes it so: to me it is a prison.

ROSENCRANTZ: Why then your ambition makes it one: 'tis too narrow for your mind.

HAMLET: O God, I could be bounded in a nut-shell, and count myself a King of infinite space; were it not that I have bad dreams.

GUILDENSTERN: Which dreams indeed are ambition: for the very substance of the ambitious, is merely the shadow of a dream.

HAMLET: A dream itself is but a shadow.

ROSENCRANTZ: Truly, and I hold ambition of so airy and light a quality, that it is but a shadow's shadow.

HAMLET: Then are our beggars bodies, and our monarchs and outstretched heroes the beggars' shadows: shall we to th' Court: for, by my fay I cannot reason.

BOTH: We'll wait upon you.

HAMLET: No such matter. I will not sort you with the rest of my servants: for to speak to you like an honest man: I am most dreadfully attended: but in the beaten way of friendship, what make you at Elsinore?

ROSENCRANTZ: To visit you my Lord, no other occasion.

HAMLET: Beggar that I am, I am even poor in thanks; but I thank you: and sure dear friends my thanks are too dear a halfpenny; were you not sent for? Is it your own inclining? Is it a free visitation? Come, deal justly with me: come, come; nay speak.

GUILDENSTERN: What should we say my Lord?

HAMLET: Why any thing. But to the purpose; you were sent for; and there is a kind of confession in your looks; which your modesties have not craft enough to colour, I know the good King and Queen have sent for you.

ROSENCRANTZ: To what end my Lord?

HAMLET: That you must teach me: but let me conjure you by the rights of our fellowship, by the consonancy of our youth, by the obligation of our ever-preserved love, and by what more dear, a better proposer could charge you withal; be even and direct with me, whether you were sent for or no.

ROSENCRANTZ: What say you?

HAMLET: Nay then I have an eye of you: if you love me hold not off.

GUILDENSTERN: My Lord, we were sent for.

HAMLET: I will tell you why; shall my anticipation prevent your discovery and your secrecy to the King and Queen, moult no feather: I have of late, but wherefore I know not, lost all my mirth, forgone all custom of exercise; and indeed, it goes so heavily with my disposition; that this goodly frame the earth, seems to me a sterile promontory; this most excellent canopy the air, look you, this brave o'er-hanging firmament, this majestical roof, fretted with golden fire: why, it appears no other thing to me, than a foul and pestilent congregation of vapours. What a piece of work is a man! how noble in reason! how infinite in faculty! in form and moving how express and admirable! in action, how like an angel! in apprehension, how like a god! the beauty of the world, the paragon of animals; and yet to me, what is this quintessence of dust? man delights not me; no, nor woman neither; though by your smiling you seem to say so.

ROSENCRANTZ: My Lord, there was no such stuff in my thoughts.

HAMLET: Why did you laugh, when I said man delights not me?

ROSENCRANTZ: To think, my Lord, if you delight not in man, what lenten entertainment the Players shall receive from you: we coted them on the way, and hither are they coming to offer you service.

HAMLET: He that plays the King shall be welcome; his Majesty shall have tribute of me: the adventurous Knight shall use his foil and target: the lover shall not sigh *gratis*; the humorous man shall end his part in peace: the Clown shall make those laugh whose lungs are tickle o' th' sere: and the lady shall say her mind freely, or the blank verse shall halt for't: what Players are they?

ROSENCRANTZ: Even those you were wont to take delight in, the tragedians of the City.

HAMLET: How chances it they travel? their residence both in reputation and profit was better both ways.

ROSENCRANTZ: I think their inhibition comes by the means of the late innovation.

HAMLET: Do they hold the same estimation they did when I was in the City? are they so follow'd?

ROSENCRANTZ: No indeed, they are not.

HAMLET: How comes it? do they grow rusty?

ROSENCRANTZ: Nay, their endeavour keeps in the wonted pace; but there is sir an aery of children, little eyases, that cry out on the top of question; and are most tyrannically clapp'd for't: these are now the fashion, and so berattle the common Stages (so they call them) that many wearing rapiers, are afraid of goose-quills, and dare scarce come thither.

HAMLET: What, are they children? who maintains 'em?

how are they escoted? Will they pursue the quality no
longer than they can sing? will they not say afterwards
if they should grow themselves to common Players (as it
is most like if their means are no better) their writers do
them wrong, to make them exclaim against their own
succession?

ROSENCRANTZ: Faith there has been much to do on both
sides: and the nation holds it no sin, to tarre them to
controversy. There was for a while, no money bid for
argument, unless the Poet and the Player went to cuffs in
the question.

HAMLET: Is't possible?

GUILDENSTERN: O there has been much throwing about
of brains.

HAMLET: Do the Boys carry it away?

ROSENCRANTZ: Ay that they do my Lord, Hercules and
his load too.

HAMLET: It is not strange: for mine uncle is King of Denmark, and those that would make mows at him while
my father lived, give twenty, forty, a hundred ducats
a-piece for his picture in little. 'Sblood there is something in this more than natural, if Philosophy could find
it out.

Flourish.

GUILDENSTERN: There are the Players.

HAMLET: Gentlemen, you are welcome to Elsinore: your
hands, come: the appurtenance of welcome, is fashion
and ceremony. Let me comply with you in the garb,
lest my extent to the Players (which I tell you must show
fairly outwards) should more appear like entertainment
than yours. You are welcome: but my uncle-father, and
aunt-mother are deceiv'd.

GUILDENSTERN: In what my dear Lord?

HAMLET: I am but mad north-north-west: when the wind is southerly, I know a hawk from a handsaw.

Enter Polonius.

POLONIUS: Well be with you gentlemen.

HAMLET: Hark you Guildenstern, and you too: at each ear a hearer: that great baby you see there, is not yet out of his swathing clouts.

ROSENCRANTZ: Happily he's the second time come to them: for they say, an old man is twice a child.

HAMLET: I will prophesy. He comes to tell me of the Players. Mark it. You say right sir: for a' Monday morning 'twas so indeed.

POLONIUS: My Lord, I have news to tell you.

HAMLET: My Lord, I have news to tell you. When Roscius was an actor in Rome —

POLONIUS: The actors are come hither my Lord.

HAMLET: Buz, buz.

POLONIUS: Upon my honour.

HAMLET: Then came each actor on his ass —

POLONIUS: The best actors in the world, either for Tragedy, Comedy, History, Pastoral, Pastoral-Comical, Historical-Pastoral: Tragical-Historical: Tragical-Comical-Historical-Pastoral: Scene individable, or Poem unlimited. Seneca cannot be too heavy, nor Plautus too light, for the law of writ, and the liberty. These are the only men.

HAMLET: O Jephthah Judge of Israel, what a treasure hadst thou ?

POLONIUS: What a treasure had he, my Lord ?

HAMLET: Why
One fair daughter, and no more,
The which he loved passing well.

POLONIUS: Still on my daughter.

HAMLET: Am I not i' th' right old Jephthah?

POLONIUS: If you call me Jephthah my Lord, I have a daughter that I love passing well.

HAMLET: Nay that follows not.

POLONIUS: What follows then, my Lord?

HAMLET: Why, as by lot, God wot: and then you know, it came to pass, as most like it was: the first row of the pious chanson will show you more. For look where my abridgements come.

Enter four or five Players.

You are welcome masters, welcome all. I am glad to see thee well: welcome good friends. O my old friend? thy face is valanced since I saw thee last: comest thou to beard me in Denmark? What, my young lady and mistress? By'r lady, your ladyship is nearer Heaven than when I saw you last, by the altitude of a chopine. Pray God your voice like a piece of uncurrent gold be not crack'd within the ring. Masters, you are welcome: we'll e'en to't like French falconers, fly at anything we see: we'll have a speech straight. Come give us a taste of your quality: come, a passionate speech.

FIRST PLAYER: What speech, my Lord?

HAMLET: I heard thee speak me a speech once, but it was never acted: or if it was, not above once, for the play I remembered pleas'd not the million, 'twas caviary to the general: but it was (as I receiv'd it, and others, whose judgements in such matters, cried in the top of mine) an excellent play; well digested in the scenes, set down with as much modesty, as cunning. I remember one said, there were no sallets in the lines, to make the matter savoury; nor no matter in the phrase, that might indict the author of affection, but call'd it an honest method. [As wholesome as sweet, and by very much more handsome than

fine.] One chief speech in it I chiefly lov'd, 'twas Æneas'
tale to Dido, and thereabout of it especially, where he
speaks of Priam's slaughter. If it live in your memory,
begin at this line, let me see, let me see:
   'The rugged Pyrrhus like th' Hyrcanian beast.'
It is not so: it begins with Pyrrhus.
   'The rugged Pyrrhus, he whose sable arms
   Black as his purpose, did the night resemble
   When he lay couched in the ominous horse,
   Hath now this dread and black complexion smear'd
   With heraldry more dismal: head to foot
   Now is he total gules, horridly trick'd
   With blood of fathers, mothers, daughters, sons,
   Bak'd and impasted with the parching streets,
   That lend a tyrannous, and damned light
   To their vile murthers, roasted in wrath and fire,
   And this o'er-sized with coagulate gore,
   With eyes like carbuncles, the hellish Pyrrhus
   Old grandsire Priam seeks.'
POLONIUS: 'Fore God, my Lord, well spoken, with good
accent, and good discretion.
FIRST PLAYER: 'Anon he finds him,
   Striking too short at Greeks. His antique sword,
   Rebellious to his arm, lies where it falls
   Repugnant to command: unequal match'd,
   Pyrrhus at Priam drives, in rage strikes wide:
   But with the whiff and wind of his fell sword,
   Th' unnerved father falls. Then senseless Ilium,
   Seeming to feel his blow, with flaming top
   Stoops to his base, and with a hideous crash
   Takes prisoner Pyrrhus' ear. For lo, his sword
   Which was declining on the milky head
   Of reverend Priam, seem'd i' th' air to stick:

So as a painted tyrant Pyrrhus stood,
And like a neutral to his will and matter,
Did nothing.
But as we often see against some storm,
A silence in the heavens, the rack stand still,
The bold winds speechless, and the orb below
As hush as death: anon the dreadful thunder
Doth rend the region. So after Pyrrhus' pause,
Aroused vengeance sets him new a-work,
And never did the Cyclops' hammers fall
On Mars his armours, forg'd for proof eterne,
With less remorse than Pyrrhus' bleeding sword
Now falls on Priam.
Out, out, thou strumpet Fortune, all you gods,
In general Synod take away her power:
Break all the spokes and fellies from her wheel,
And bowl the round nave down the hill of Heaven,
As low as to the fiends.'

POLONIUS: This is too long.

HAMLET: It shall to th' barber's, with your beard. Prithee
say on: he's for a jig, or a tale of bawdry, or he sleeps.
Say on; come to Hecuba.

FIRST PLAYER: 'But who, O who, had seen the mobled
Queen.'

HAMLET: 'The mobled Queen?'

POLONIUS: That's good: 'mobled Queen' is good.

FIRST PLAYER: 'Run barefoot up and down, threatening
the flame
With bisson rheum: a clout about that head
Where late the diadem stood, and for a robe
About her lank and all o'er-teemed loins,
A blanket in th' alarum of fear caught up.
Who this had seen, with tongue in venom steep'd,

> 'Gainst Fortune's state, would treason have pro-
> nounc'd;
> But if the gods themselves did see her then,
> When she saw Pyrrhus make malicious sport
> In mincing with his sword her husband's limbs,
> The instant burst of clamour that she made
> (Unless things mortal move them not at all)
> Would have made milch the burning eyes of Heaven,
> And passion in the gods.'

POLONIUS: Look whe'er he has not turn'd his colour, and
has tears in's eyes. Pray you no more.

HAMLET: 'Tis well, I'll have thee speak out the rest, soon.
Good my Lord, will you see the Players well bestow'd.
Do you hear, let them be well us'd: for they are the
abstracts and brief chronicles of the time. After your
death, you were better have a bad epitaph, than their ill
report while you live.

POLONIUS: My Lord, I will use them according to their
desert.

HAMLET: God's bodykins man, better. Use every man
after his desert, and who should 'scape whipping? Use
them after your own honour and dignity. The less they
deserve, the more merit is in your bounty. Take them in.

POLONIUS: Come sirs.

HAMLET: Follow him friends: we'll hear a play to-morrow
Exit Polonius and Players except the First Player. Dost thou
hear me old friend, can you play the Murther of Gonzago?

FIRST PLAYER: Ay my lord.

HAMLET: We'll ha't to-morrow night. You could for a
need study a speech of some dozen or sixteen lines
which I would set down, and insert in't? could you not?

FIRST PLAYER: Ay my Lord.

HAMLET: Very well. Follow that Lord, and look you mock

him not. My good friends, I'll leave you till night, you
are welcome to Elsinore.

ROSENCRANTZ: Good my Lord.

Exeunt.

Manet Hamlet.

HAMLET: Ay so, God buy ye: now I am alone.
Oh what a rogue and peasant slave am I!
Is it not monstrous that this Player here,
But in a fiction, in a dream of passion,
Could force his soul so to his whole conceit,
That from her working, all his visage wann'd;
Tears in his eyes, distraction in 's aspect,
A broken voice, and his whole function suiting
With forms, to his conceit? and all for nothing?
For Hecuba?
What's Hecuba to him, or he to Hecuba,
That he should weep for her? What would he do,
Had he the motive and the cue for passion
That I have? He would drown the stage with tears,
And cleave the general ear with horrid speech:
Make mad the guilty, and appal the free,
Confound the ignorant, and amaze indeed,
The very faculty of eyes and ears. Yet I,
A dull and muddy-mettled rascal, peak
Like John-a-dreams, unpregnant of my cause,
And can say nothing: no, not for a King,
Upon whose property, and most dear life,
A damn'd defeat was made. Am I a coward?
Who calls me villain? breaks my pate across?
Plucks off my beard, and blows it in my face?
Tweaks me by th' nose? gives me the lie i' th' throat,
As deep as to the lungs? who does me this?
Ha? Why, I should take it: for it cannot be,

But I am pigeon-liver'd, and lack gall
To make oppression bitter, or ere this,
I should have fatted all the region kites
With this slave's offal, bloody, bawdy villain,
Remorseless, treacherous, lecherous, kindless villain!
O Vengeance!
Why, what an ass am I? Ay sure, this is most brave,
That I, the son of the dear murthered,
Prompted to my revenge by Heaven, and Hell,
Must (like a whore) unpack my heart with words,
And fall a-cursing like a very drab.
A scullion! Fie upon't: foh. About my brain.
I have heard, that guilty creatures sitting at a play,
Have by the very cunning of the scene,
Been struck so to the soul, that presently
They have proclaim'd their malefactions.
For murther, though it have no tongue, will speak
With most miraculous organ. I'll have these Players,
Play something like the murder of my father,
Before mine uncle. I'll observe his looks,
I'll tent him to the quick: if he but blench
I know my course. The spirit that I have seen
May be the Devil, and the Devil hath power
T' assume a pleasing shape, yea and perhaps
Out of my weakness, and my melancholy,
As he is very potent with such spirits,
Abuses me to damn me. I'll have grounds
More relative than this: the play's the thing,
Wherein I'll catch the conscience of the King.

Exit.

III. 1

Enter King, Queen, Polonius, Ophelia, Rosencrantz,
Guildenstern, and Lords.

KING: And can you by no drift of circumstance
Get from him why he puts on this confusion,
Grating so harshly all his days of quiet
With turbulent and dangerous lunacy?

ROSENCRANTZ: He does confess he feels himself distracted,
But from what cause he will by no means speak.

GUILDENSTERN: Nor do we find him forward to be
sounded,
But with a crafty madness keeps aloof,
When we would bring him on to some confession
Of his true state.

QUEEN: Did he receive you well?

ROSENCRANTZ: Most like a gentleman.

GUILDENSTERN: But with much forcing of his disposition.

ROSENCRANTZ: Niggard of question, but of our demands
Most free in his reply.

QUEEN: Did you assay him to any pastime?

ROSENCRANTZ: Madam, it so fell out, that certain Players
We o'er-raught on the way: of these we told him,
And there did seem in him a kind of joy
To hear of it: they are about the Court,
And (as I think) they have already order
This night to play before him.

POLONIUS: 'Tis most true:
And he beseech'd me to entreat your Majesties
To hear, and see the matter.

KING: With all my heart, and it doth much content me
To hear him so inclin'd.

Good gentlemen, give him a further edge,
And drive his purpose on to these delights.

ROSENCRANTZ: We shall my Lord.

Exeunt Rosencrantz and Guildenstern.

KING: Sweet Gertrude leave us too,
For we have closely sent for Hamlet hither,
That he, as 'twere by accident, may here
Affront Ophelia.
Her father, and myself (lawful espials),
Will, so bestow ourselves, that seeing unseen
We may of their encounter frankly judge,
And gather by him, as he is behav'd,
If 't be th' affliction of his love, or no,
That thus he suffers for.

QUEEN: I shall obey you,
And for your part Ophelia, I do wish
That your good beauties be the happy cause
Of Hamlet's wildness: so shall I hope your virtues
Will bring him to his wonted way again,
To both your honours.

OPHELIA: Madam, I wish it may.

Exit Queen.

POLONIUS: Ophelia, walk you here. Gracious so please
you
We will bestow ourselves: read on this book,
That show of such an exercise may colour
Your loneliness. We are oft to blame in this,
'Tis too much prov'd, that with Devotion's visage,
And pious action, we do sugar o'er
The devil himself.

KING: O 'tis too true!
How smart a lash that speech doth give my conscience!
The harlot's cheek beautied with plastering art

Is not more ugly to the thing that helps it,
Than is my deed, to my most painted word.
O heavy burthen!
POLONIUS: I hear him coming, let's withdraw my Lord.
Exeunt.
Enter Hamlet.
HAMLET: To be, or not to be, that is the question:
Whether 'tis nobler in the mind to suffer
The slings and arrows of outrageous Fortune,
Or to take arms against a sea of troubles,
And by opposing end them: to die to sleep;
No more; and by a sleep, to say we end
The heart-ache, and the thousand natural shocks
That flesh is heir to? 'tis a consummation
Devoutly to be wish'd. To die to sleep,
To sleep, perchance to dream; ay, there's the rub,
For in that sleep of death, what dreams may come,
When we have shuffled off this mortal coil,
Must give us pause. There's the respect
That makes calamity of so long life:
For who would bear the whips and `scorns of time,
The oppressor's wrong, the proud man's contumely,
The pangs of dispiz'd love, the Law's delay,
The insolence of office, and the spurns
That patient merit of the unworthy takes,
When he himself might his quietus make,
With a bare bodkin? who would fardels bear,
To grunt and sweat under a weary life,
But that the dread of something after death,
The undiscovered country, from whose bourn
No traveller returns, puzzles the will,
And makes us rather bear those ills we have,
Than fly to others that we know not of.

Thus conscience does make cowards of us all,
And thus the native hue of resolution
Is sicklied o'er, with the pale cast of thought,
And enterprises of great pith and moment,
With this regard their currents turn awry,
And lose the name of action. Soft you now,
The fair Ophelia? Nymph, in thy orisons
Be all my sins remember'd.

OPHELIA: Good my Lord,
How does your honour for this many a day?

HAMLET: I humbly thank you: well, well, well.

OPHELIA: My Lord, I have remembrances of yours,
That I have longed long to re-deliver.
I pray you now, receive them.

HAMLET: No, no, I never gave you aught.

OPHELIA: My honour'd Lord, I know right well you
did,
And with them words of so sweet breath compos'd,
As made the things more rich, their perfume left:
Take these again, for to the noble mind,
Rich gifts wax poor, when givers prove unkind.
There my Lord.

HAMLET: Ha, ha: are you honest?

OPHELIA: My Lord.

HAMLET: Are you fair?

OPHELIA: What means your Lordship?

HAMLET: That if you be honest and fair, your honesty
should admit no discourse to your beauty.

OPHELIA: Could beauty my Lord, have better commerce
than with honesty?

HAMLET: Ay, truly: for the power of beauty will sooner
transform honesty from what it is, to a bawd, than the
force of honesty can translate beauty into his likeness.

This was sometime a paradox, but now the time gives it proof. I did love you once.

OPHELIA: Indeed my Lord, you made me believe so.

HAMLET: You should not have believed me. For virtue, cannot so inoculate our old stock, but we shall relish of it. I loved you not.

OPHELIA: I was the more deceived.

HAMLET: Get thee to a nunnery. Why wouldst thou be a breeder of sinners? I am myself indifferent honest, but yet I could accuse me of such things, that it were better my mother had not borne me. I am very proud, revengeful, ambitious, with more offences at my beck, than I have thoughts to put them in, imagination to give them shape, or time to act them in. What should such fellows as I do, crawling between Heaven and earth. We are arrant knaves all, believe none of us. Go thy ways to a nunnery. Where's your father?

OPHELIA: At home, my Lord.

HAMLET: Let the doors be shut upon him, that he may play the fool no where but in's own house. Farewell.

OPHELIA: O help him, you sweet Heavens.

HAMLET: If thou dost marry, I'll give thee this plague for thy dowry. Be thou as chaste as ice, as pure as snow, thou shalt not escape calumny. Get thee to a nunnery. Go, farewell. Or, if thou wilt needs marry, marry a fool: for wise men know well enough, what monsters you make of them. To a nunnery go, and quickly too. Farewell.

OPHELIA: O heavenly powers, restore him.

HAMLET: I have heard of your paintings too well enough. God has given you one face, and you make yourselves another: you jig, you amble, and you lisp, and nickname God's creatures, and make your wantonness, your

ignorance. Go to, I'll no more on't, it hath made me mad.
I say, we will have no more marriages. Those that are
married already, all but one shall live, the rest shall keep
as they are. To a nunnery, go.

Exit Hamlet.

OPHELIA: O what a noble mind is here o'erthrown!
The courtier's, soldier's, scholar's eye, tongue, sword,
Th' expectancy and rose of the fair State,
The glass of fashion, and the mould of form,
Th' observ'd of all observers, quite, quite down.
And I of ladies most deject and wretched,
That suck'd the honey of his music vows;
Now see that noble, and most sovereign reason,
Like sweet bells jangled out of tune, and harsh,
That unmatch'd form and feature of blown youth,
Blasted with ecstasy. O woe is me,
T' have seen what I have seen: see what I see.

Enter King and Polonius.

KING: Love? his affections do not that way tend,
Nor what he spake, though it lack'd form a little,
Was not like madness. There's something in his soul,
O'er which his melancholy sits on brood,
And I do doubt the hatch, and the disclose
Will be some danger, which for to prevent
I have in quick determination
Thus set it down. He shall with speed to England
For the demand of our neglected tribute:
Haply the seas and countries different
With variable objects, shall expel
This something-settled matter in his heart:
Whereon his brains still beating puts him thus
From fashion of himself. What think you on't?

POLONIUS: It shall do well. But yet do I believe

The origin and commencement of his grief
Sprung from neglected love. How now Ophelia:
You need not tell us, what Lord Hamlet said,
We heard it all. My Lord, do as you please,
But if you hold it fit after the play,
Let his Queen mother all alone entreat him
To show his grief: let her be round with him
And I'll be plac'd, so please you, in the ear
Of all their conference. If she find him not,
To England send him: or confine him where
Your wisdom best shall think.

KING: It shall be so:
Madness in great ones, must not unwatch'd go.
Exeunt.

III.2

Enter Hamlet, and two or three of the Players.

HAMLET: Speak the speech I pray you as I pronounc'd it
to you trippingly on the tongue: but if you mouth it, as
many of your Players do, I had as lief the town-crier had
spoke my lines: nor do not saw the air too much with
your hand thus, but use all gently; for in the very tor-
rent, tempest, and (as I may say) the whirlwind of passion, you must acquire and beget a temperance that may
give it smoothness. O it offends me to the soul, to hear
a robustious periwig-pated fellow tear a passion to tat-
ters, to very rags, to split the ears of the groundlings;
who (for the most part) are capable of nothing, but inexplicable dumb-shows, and noise: I could have such a
fellow whipped for o'erdoing Termagant: it out-herods
Herod. Pray you avoid it.

PLAYER: I warrant your Honour.

HAMLET: Be not too tame neither: but let your own discretion be your tutor.   Suit the action to the word, the word to the action, with this special observance: that you o'erstep not the modesty of Nature: for any thing so overdone, is from the purpose of playing, whose end both at the first and now, was and is, to hold as 'twere the mirror up to Nature; to show Virtue her own feature, Scorn her own image, and the very age and body of the time, his form and pressure. Now, this overdone, or come tardy off, though it make the unskilful laugh, cannot but make the judicious grieve; the censure of the which one, must in your allowance o'erweigh a whole theatre of others. Oh, there be Players that I have seen play, and heard others praise, and that highly (not to speak it profanely) that neither having the accent of Christians, nor the gait of Christian, pagan, nor man, have so strutted and bellowed, that I have thought some of Nature's journeymen had made men, and not made them well, they imitated humanity so abominably.

FIRST PLAYER: I hope we have reform'd that indifferently with us, sir.

HAMLET: O reform it altogether. And let those that play your Clowns, speak no more than is set down for them. For there be of them, that will themselves laugh, to set on some quantity of barren spectators to laugh too, though in the mean time, some necessary question of the play be then to be considered: that's villainous, and shows a most pitiful ambition in the Fool that uses it. Go make you ready.

Exeunt Players.
Enter Polonius, Rosencrantz, and Guildenstern.

How now my Lord, will the King hear this piece of work?

POLONIUS: And the Queen too, and that presently.
HAMLET: Bid the Players make haste.
                    Exit Polonius.
  Will you two help to hasten them?
BOTH: We will my Lord.
                    Exeunt.
                    Enter Horatio.
HAMLET: What ho, Horatio?
HORATIO: Here sweet Lord, at your service.
HAMLET: Horatio, thou art e'en as just a man
  As e'er my conversation cop'd withal.
HORATIO: O my dear Lord.
HAMLET: Nay, do not think I flatter:
  For what advancement may I hope from thee,
  That no revenue hast, but thy good spirits
  To feed and clothe thee? Why should the poor be
    flatter'd?
  No, let the candied tongue, lick absurd pomp,
  And crook the pregnant hinges of the knee,
  Where thrift may follow fawning; dost thou hear,
  Since my dear soul was mistress of my choice,
  And could of men distinguish, her election
  Hath seal'd thee for herself. For thou hast been
  As one in suffering all, that suffers nothing.
  A man that Fortune's buffets, and rewards
  Hath ta'en with equal thanks. And blest are those,
  Whose blood and judgement are so well commingled,
  That they are not a pipe for Fortune's finger,
  To sound what stop she please. Give me that man,
  That is not passion's slave, and I will wear him
  In my heart's core, ay, in my heart of heart,
  As I do thee. Something too much of this.
  There is a play to-night before the King;

One scene of it comes near the circumstance
Which I have told thee, of my father's death.
I prithee, when thou seest that act afoot,
Even with the very comment of thy soul
Observe mine uncle: if his occulted guilt,
Do not itself unkennel in one speech,
It is a damned ghost that we have seen:
And my imaginations are as foul
As Vulcan's stithy. Give him heedful note,
For I mine eyes will rivet to his face:
And after we will both our judgements join,
To censure of his seeming.

HORATIO: Well, my Lord.
If he steal aught the whilst this play is playing,
And 'scape detecting, I will pay the theft.

Enter trumpets and kettledrums.

HAMLET: They are coming to the play: I must be idle.
Get you a place.

*Enter King, Queen, Polonius, Ophelia, Rosencrantz, Guilden-
stern, and other Lords attendant, with his Guard carrying
torches. Danish March. Sound a flourish.*

KING: How fares our Cousin Hamlet?

HAMLET: Excellent i' faith, of the chameleon's dish: I eat
the air, promise-cramm'd, you cannot feed capons so.

KING: I have nothing with this answer Hamlet, these words
are not mine.

HAMLET: No, nor mine. Now my Lord, you played once
i' th' university, you say?

POLONIUS: That I did my Lord, and was accounted a good
actor.

HAMLET: What did you enact?

POLONIUS: I did enact Julius Cæsar, I was kill'd i' th'
Capitol: Brutus kill'd me.

HAMLET: It was a brute part of him, to kill so capital a calf there. Be the Players ready?

ROSENCRANTZ: Ay my Lord, they stay upon your patience.

QUEEN: Come hither my good Hamlet, sit by me.

HAMLET: No, good mother, here's metal more attractive.

POLONIUS: O ho, do you mark that?

HAMLET: Lady, shall I lie in your lap?

OPHELIA: No, my Lord.

HAMLET: I mean, my head upon your lap?

OPHELIA: Ay, my Lord.

HAMLET: Do you think I meant country matters?

OPHELIA: I think nothing, my Lord.

HAMLET: That's a fair thought to lie between maids' legs.

OPHELIA: What is, my Lord?

HAMLET: Nothing.

OPHELIA: You are merry, my Lord?

HAMLET: Who I?

OPHELIA: Ay, my Lord.

HAMLET: O God, your only jig-maker: what should a man do, but be merry? for look you how cheerfully my mother looks, and my father died within's two hours.

OPHELIA: Nay, 'tis twice two months, my Lord.

HAMLET: So long? Nay then let the Devil wear black, for I'll have a suit of sables. O Heavens! die two months ago, and not forgotten yet? Then there's hope, a great man's memory, may outlive his life half a year: but by'r lady he must build churches then: or else shall he suffer not thinking on, with the hobby-horse, whose epitaph is, 'For O, for O, the hobby-horse is forgot.'

Hautboys play. The dumb-show enters.

Enter a King and Queen, very lovingly; the Queen embracing him and he her. She kneels and makes show of protestation unto him. He takes her up, and declines his head upon her neck; lays him down upon a bank of flowers. She seeing him asleep, leaves him. Anon comes in a fellow, takes off his crown, kisses it, and pours poison in the King's ears, and exits. The Queen returns, finds the King dead, and makes passionate action. The Poisoner, with some two or three Mutes comes in again, seeming to lament with her. The dead body is carried away: the Poisoner wooes the Queen with gifts, she seems loath and unwilling awhile, but in the end accepts his love.

Exeunt.

OPHELIA: What means this, my Lord?

HAMLET: Marry this is miching mallecho, that means mischief.

OPHELIA: Belike this show imports the argument of the play.

HAMLET: We shall know by these fellows: the Players cannot keep counsel: they'll tell all.

OPHELIA: Will he tell us what this show meant?

HAMLET: Ay, or any show that you will show him. Be not you ashamed to show, he'll not shame to tell you what it means.

OPHELIA: You are naught, you are naught, I'll mark the play.

Enter Prologue.

PROLOGUE: For us, and for our tragedy,
            Here stooping to your clemency:
            We beg your hearing patiently.

Exit.

HAMLET: Is this a prologue, or the posy of a ring?

OPHELIA: 'Tis brief, my Lord.

HAMLET: As woman's love.
   Enter two Players, King and his Queen.
PLAYER KING: Full thirty times hath Phœbus' cart gone
 round,
 Neptune's salt wash, and Tellus' orbed ground:
 And thirty dozen Moons with borrow'd sheen,
 About the world have times twelve thirties been,
 Since love our hearts, and Hymen did our hands
 Unite commutual, in most sacred bands.
PLAYER QUEEN: So many journeys may the Sun and
 Moon
 Make us again count o'er, ere love be done.
 But woe is me, you are so sick of late,
 So far from cheer, and from your former state
 That I distrust you: yet though I distrust,
 Discomfort you, my Lord, it nothing must:
 For women's fear and love, holds quantity,
 In neither aught, or in extremity:
 Now what my love is, proof hath made you know,
 And as my love is siz'd, my fear is so:
 [Where love is great, the littlest doubts are fear,
 Where little fears grow great, great love grows there.]
PLAYER KING: Faith I must leave thee love, and shortly
 too:
 My operant powers their functions leave to do:
 And thou shalt live in this fair world behind,
 Honour'd, belov'd, and haply, one as kind
 For husband shalt thou —
PLAYER QUEEN: O confound the rest:
 Such love, must needs be treason in my breast:
 In second husband let me be accurst,
 None wed the second, but who kill'd the first.
HAMLET: Wormwood, wormwood.

PLAYER QUEEN: The instances that second marriage
    move,
Are base respects of thrift, but none of love.
A second time, I kill my husband dead,
When second husband kisses me in bed.

PLAYER KING: I do believe you think what now you
    speak:
But what we do determine, oft we break:
Purpose is but the slave to memory,
Of violent birth, but poor validity:
Which now like fruit unripe sticks on the tree,
But fall unshaken, when they mellow be.
Most necessary 'tis, that we forget
To pay ourselves, what to ourselves is debt:
What to ourselves in passion we propose,
The passion ending, doth the purpose lose.
The violence of either grief or joy,
Their own enactures with themselves destroy:
Where joy most revels, grief doth most lament;
Grief joys, joy grieves on slender accident.
This world is not for aye, nor 'tis not strange
That even our loves should with our fortunes change.
For 'tis a question left us yet to prove,
Whether Love lead Fortune, or else Fortune Love.
The great man down, you mark his favourite flies,
The poor advanc'd, makes friends of enemies:
And hitherto doth Love on Fortune tend,
For who not needs, shall never lack a friend:
And who in want a hollow friend doth try,
Directly seasons him his enemy.
But orderly to end, where I begun,
Our wills and fates do so contrary run,
That our devices still are overthrown,

Our thoughts are ours, their ends none of our own.
So think thou wilt no second husband wed:
But die thy thoughts, when thy first Lord is dead.

PLAYER QUEEN: Nor earth to me give food, nor Heaven
      light,
Sport and repose lock from me day and night:
[To desperation turn my trust and hope,
An anchor's cheer in prison be my scope:]
Each opposite that blanks the face of joy,
Meet what I would have well, and it destroy:
Both here, and hence, pursue me lasting strife,
If once a widow, ever I be wife.

HAMLET: If she should break it now.

PLAYER KING: 'Tis deeply sworn: sweet, leave me here
      awhile,
My spirits grow dull, and fain I would beguile
The tedious day with sleep.

Sleeps.

PLAYER QUEEN: Sleep rock thy brain,
And never come mischance between us twain.

Exit.

HAMLET: Madam, how like you this play?

QUEEN: The lady protests too much methinks.

HAMLET: O but she'll keep her word.

KING: Have you heard the argument? Is there no offence
in't?

HAMLET: No, no, they do but jest, poison in jest, no offence
i' th' world.

KING: What do you call the play?

HAMLET: The Mouse-trap: marry how? Tropically: this
play is the image of a murder done in Vienna: Gonzago
is the Duke's name, his wife Baptista: you shall see anon:
'tis a knavish piece of work: but what o' that? your

Majesty, and we that have free souls, it touches us not:
let the gall'd jade winch, our withers are unwrung.

Enter Lucianus.

This is one Lucianus nephew to the King.

OPHELIA: You are a good Chorus, my Lord.

HAMLET: I could interpret between you and your love: if
I could see the puppets dallying.

OPHELIA: You are keen my Lord, you are keen.

HAMLET: It would cost you a groaning, to take off my
edge.

OPHELIA: Still better and worse.

HAMLET: So you must take husbands. Begin murderer.
Pox, leave thy damnable faces, and begin. Come, the
croaking raven doth bellow for revenge.

LUCIANUS: Thoughts black, hands apt, drugs fit, and time
agreeing:
Confederate season, else, no creature seeing:
Thou mixture rank, of midnight weeds collected,
With Hecat's ban, thrice blasted, thrice infected,
Thy natural magic, and dire property,
On wholesome life, usurp immediately.

Pours the poison in his ears.

HAMLET: He poisons him i' th' garden for 's estate: his
name's Gonzago: the story is extant and writ in choice
Italian. You shall see anon how the murtherer gets the
love of Gonzago's wife.

OPHELIA: The King rises.

HAMLET: What, frighted with false fire?

QUEEN: How fares my Lord?

POLONIUS: Give o'er the play.

KING: Give me some light. Away.

ALL: Lights, lights, lights.

Exeunt all but Hamlet and Horatio.

HAMLET: Why let the stricken deer go weep,
   The hart ungalled play:
For some must watch, while some must sleep;
   So runs the world away.
Would not this sir, and a forest of feathers, if the rest of
my fortunes turn Turk with me, with two Provincial
roses on my raz'd shoes, get me a fellowship in a cry of
Players, sir?

HORATIO: Half a share.

HAMLET: A whole one I,
For thou dost know: O Damon dear,
   This realm dismantled was
Of Jove himself, and now reigns here
   A very very pajock.

HORATIO: You might have rhymed.

HAMLET: Oh good Horatio, I'll take the Ghost's word for
a thousand pound. Didst perceive?

HORATIO: Very well my Lord.

HAMLET: Upon the talk of the poisoning?

HORATIO: I did very well note him.
     Enter Rosencrantz and Guildenstern.

HAMLET: Oh, ha? Come some music. Come the re-
corders:
   For if the King like not the comedy,
   Why then belike he likes it not perdy.
Come some music.

GUILDENSTERN: Good my Lord, vouchsafe me a word
with you.

HAMLET: Sir, a whole history.

GUILDENSTERN: The King, sir.

HAMLET: Ay sir, what of him?

GUILDENSTERN: Is in his retirement, marvellous distemper'd.

HAMLET: With drink sir?

GUILDENSTERN: No my Lord, rather with choler.

HAMLET: Your wisdom should show itself more richer, to signify this to his doctor: for, for me to put him to his purgation, would perhaps plunge him into far more choler.

GUILDENSTERN: Good my Lord put your discourse into some frame, and start not so wildly from my affair.

HAMLET: I am tame sir, pronounce.

GUILDENSTERN: The Queen your mother, in most great affliction of spirit, hath sent me to you.

HAMLET: You are welcome.

GUILDENSTERN: Nay, good my Lord, this courtesy is not of the right breed. If it shall please you to make me a wholesome answer, I will do your mother's commandment: if not, your pardon, and my return shall be the end of my business.

HAMLET: Sir, I cannot.

GUILDENSTERN: What, my Lord?

HAMLET: Make you a wholesome answer: my wit's diseased. But, sir, such answer as I can make, you shall command: or rather as you say, my mother: therefore no more but to the matter. My mother you say —

ROSENCRANTZ: Then thus she says: your behaviour hath struck her into amazement, and admiration.

HAMLET: O wonderful son, that can so astonish a mother. But is there no sequel at the heels of this mother's admiration?

ROSENCRANTZ: She desires to speak with you in her closet, ere you go to bed.

HAMLET: We shall obey, were she ten times our mother. Have you any further trade with us?

ROSENCRANTZ: My Lord, you once did love me.

HAMLET: So I do still, by these pickers and stealers.

ROSENCRANTZ: Good my Lord, what is your cause of distemper? you do surely bar the door of your own liberty, if you deny your griefs to your friend.

HAMLET: Sir I lack advancement.

ROSENCRANTZ: How can that be, when you have the voice of the king himself, for your succession in Denmark?

HAMLET: Ay, but while the grass grows, the proverb is something musty.

Enter one with a recorder.

O the recorder. Let me see, to withdraw with you, why do you go about to recover the wind of me, as if you would drive me into a toil?

GUILDENSTERN: O my Lord, if my duty be too bold, my love is too unmannerly.

HAMLET: I do not well understand that. Will you play upon this pipe?

GUILDENSTERN: My Lord, I cannot.

HAMLET: I pray you.

GUILDENSTERN: Believe me, I cannot.

HAMLET: I do beseech you.

GUILDENSTERN: I know no touch of it, my Lord.

HAMLET: 'Tis as easy as lying: govern these ventages with your finger and thumb, give it breath with your mouth, and it will discourse most eloquent music. Look you, these are the stops.

GUILDENSTERN: But these cannot I command to any utterance of harmony, I have not the skill.

HAMLET: Why look you now, how unworthy a thing you make of me: you would play upon me; you would seem to know my stops: you would pluck out the heart of my mystery; you would sound me from my lowest

note, to the top of my compass: and there is much music,
excellent voice, in this little organ, yet cannot you make
it speak. Why do you think that I am easier to be played
on, than a pipe? Call me what instrument you will,
though you can fret me, you cannot play upon me.
God bless you sir.

Enter Polonius.

POLONIUS: My Lord; the Queen would speak with you,
and presently.

HAMLET: Do you see that cloud? that's almost in shape
like a camel.

POLONIUS: By th' mass, and it's like a camel indeed.

HAMLET: Methinks it is like a weazel.

POLONIUS: It is back'd like a weazel.

HAMLET: Or like a whale?

POLONIUS: Very like a whale.

HAMLET: Then I will come to my mother, by and by;
They fool me to the top of my bent. I will come by and
by.

POLONIUS: I will say so.

Exit.

HAMLET: By and by, is easily said. Leave me friends:

Exeunt all but Hamlet.

'Tis now the very witching time of night,
When churchyards yawn, and Hell itself breathes out
Contagion to this world. Now could I drink hot blood,
And do such bitter business as the day
Would quake to look on. Soft now, to my mother:
O heart, lose not thy nature; let not ever
The soul of Nero, enter this firm bosom:
Let me be cruel, not unnatural.
I will speak daggers to her, but use none:
My tongue and soul in this be hypocrites.

How in my words, somever she be shent,
To give them seals, never my soul consent.
Exit.

III. 3

Enter King, Rosencrantz, and Guildenstern.

KING: I like him not, nor stands it safe with us,
To let his madness range. Therefore prepare you,
I your commission will forthwith dispatch,
And he to England shall along with you:
The terms of our estate, may not endure
Hazard so dangerous as doth hourly grow
Out of his lunacies.

GUILDENSTERN: We will ourselves provide:
Most holy and religious fear it is
To keep those many many bodies safe
That live and feed upon your Majesty.

ROSENCRANTZ: The single and peculiar life is bound
With all the strength and armour of the mind,
To keep itself fron noyance; but much more,
That spirit, upon whose weal depends and rests
The lives of many; the cease of Majesty
Dies not alone, but like a gulf doth draw
What's near it, with it. It is a massy wheel
Fix'd on the summit of the highest mount,
To whose huge spokes, ten thousand lesser things
Are mortis'd and adjoin'd: which when it falls,
Each small annexment, petty consequence
Attends the boisterous ruin. Never alone
Did the King sigh, but with a general groan.

KING: Arm you, I pray you to this speedy voyage;
For we will fetters put upon this fear,

Which now goes too free-footed.

BOTH: We will haste us.

Exeunt.

Enter Polonius.

POLONIUS: My Lord, he's going to his mother's closet:
Behind the arras I'll convey myself
To hear the process. I'll warrant she'll tax him home,
And as you said, and wisely was it said,
'Tis meet that some more audience than a mother,
Since Nature makes them partial, should o'erhear
The speech of vantage. Fare you well my Liege,
I'll call upon you ere you go to bed,
And tell you what I know.

KING: Thanks dear my Lord.

Exit Polonius.

Oh my offence is rank, it smells to Heaven,
It hath the primal eldest curse upon 't,
A brother's murther. Pray can I not,
Though inclination be as sharp as will:
My stronger guilt, defeats my strong intent,
And like a man to double business bound,
I stand in pause where I shall first begin,
And both neglect; what if this cursed hand
Were thicker than itself with brother's blood,
Is there not rain enough in the sweet heavens
To wash it white as snow? Whereto serves mercy,
But to confront the visage of offence?
And what's in prayer, but this twofold force,
To be forestalled ere we come to fall,
Or pardon'd being down? Then I'll look up,
My fault is past. But oh, what form of prayer
Can serve my turn? Forgive me my foul murther:
That cannot be, since I am still possess'd

Of those effects for which I did the murther,
My crown, mine own ambition, and my Queen.
May one be pardon'd, and retain th' offence?
In the corrupted currents of this world,
Offence's gilded hand may shove by Justice,
And oft 'tis seen, the wicked prize itself
Buys out the Law; but 'tis not so above,
There is no shuffling, there the action lies
In his true nature, and we ourselves compell'd
Even to the teeth and forehead of our faults,
To give in evidence. What then? what rests?
Try what repentance can. What can it not?
Yet what can it, when one cannot repent?
O wretched state! O bosom, black as death!
O limed soul, that struggling to be free,
Art more engag'd; help angels, make assay:
Bow stubborn knees, and heart with strings of steel,
Be soft as sinews of the new-born babe,
All may be well.

Enter Hamlet.

HAMLET: Now might I do it pat, now he is praying,
And now I'll do't, and so he goes to Heaven,
And so am I reveng'd: that would be scann'd,
A villain kills my father, and for that
I his sole son, do this same villain send
To Heaven.
O this is hire and salary, not revenge.
He took my father grossly, full of bread,
With all his crimes broad blown, as flush as May,
And how his audit stands, who knows, save Heaven:
But in our circumstance and course of thought
'Tis heavy with him; and am I then reveng'd,
To take him in the purging of his soul,

When he is fit and season'd for his passage?
No.
Up sword, and know thou a more horrid hent
When he is drunk asleep: or in his rage,
Or in th' incestuous pleasure of his bed,
At gaming, swearing, or about some act
That has no relish of salvation in't,
Then trip him, that his heels may kick at Heaven,
And that his soul may be as damn'd and black
As Hell, whereto it goes. My mother stays,
This physic but prolongs thy sickly days.

Exit.

KING: My words fly up, my thoughts remain below,
Words without thoughts, never to Heaven go.

III. 4

Enter Queen and Polonius.

POLONIUS: He will come straight: look you lay home to
   him,
   Tell him his pranks have been too broad to bear with,
   And that your Grace hath screen'd, and stood between
   Much heat, and him. I'll silence me e'en here:
   Pray you be round with him.

HAMLET: Mother, mother, mother.

QUEEN: I'll warrant you, fear me not. Withdraw, I hear
   him coming.

Enter Hamlet.

HAMLET: Now mother, what's the matter?

QUEEN: Hamlet, thou hast thy father much offended.

HAMLET: Mother, you have my father much offended.

QUEEN: Come, come, you answer with an idle tongue.

HAMLET: Go, go, you question with an idle tongue.

QUEEN: Why how now Hamlet?

HAMLET: What's the matter now?

QUEEN: Have you forgot me?

HAMLET: No by the Rood, not so:
  You are the Queen, your husband's brother's wife,
  But would you were not so. You are my mother.

QUEEN: Nay, then I'll set those to you that can speak.

HAMLET: Come, come, and sit you down, you shall not
    budge:
  You go not till I set you up a glass,
  Where you may see the inmost part of you.

QUEEN: What wilt thou do? thou wilt not murder me?
  Help, help, hoa.

POLONIUS: What hoa, help, help, help.

HAMLET: How now, a rat? dead for a ducat, dead.

                    Kills Polonius.

POLONIUS: O I am slain.

QUEEN: O me, what hast thou done?

HAMLET: Nay I know not, is it the King?

QUEEN: O what a rash, and bloody deed is this!

HAMLET: A bloody deed, almost as bad good mother,
  As kill a King, and marry with his brother.

QUEEN: As kill a King?

HAMLET: Ay Lady, 'twas my word.
  Thou wretched, rash, intruding fool, farewell.
  I took thee for thy better: take thy fortune,
  Thou find'st to be too busy, is some danger.
  Leave wringing of your hands, peace, sit you down,
  And let me wring your heart, for so I shall
  If it be made of penetrable stuff;
  If damned custom have not braz'd it so,
  That it is proof and bulwark against sense.

QUEEN: What have I done, that thou darest wag thy tongue

In noise so rude against me?
HAMLET: Such an act
That blurs the grace and blush of Modesty,
Calls Virtue hypocrite, takes off the rose
From the fair forehead of an innocent love,
And sets a blister there, makes marriage-vows
As false as dicers' oaths. O such a deed,
As from the body of contraction plucks
The very soul, and sweet Religion makes
A rhapsody of words. Heaven's face doth glow,
Yea this solidity and compound mass,
With tristful visage as against the doom,
Is thought-sick at the act.
QUEEN: Ay me; what act,
That roars so loud, and thunders in the index?
HAMLET: Look here upon this picture, and on this,
The counterfeit presentment of two brothers:
See what a grace was seated on this brow,
Hyperion's curls, the front of Jove himself,
An eye like Mars, to threaten or command,
A station like the herald Mercury,
New-lighted on a heaven-kissing hill:
A combination, and a form indeed,
Where every god did seem to set his seal,
To give the world assurance of a man.
This was your husband. Look you now what follows.
Here is your husband, like a mildew'd ear
Blasting his wholesome breath. Have you eyes?
Could you on this fair mountain leave to feed,
And batten on this moor? Ha? have you eyes?
You cannot call it love: for at your age,
The hey-day in the blood is tame, it's humble,
And waits upon the judgement: and what judgement

Would step from this, to this? [Sense sure you have,
Else could you not have motion, but sure that sense
Is apoplex'd, for madness would not err,
Nor sense to ecstasy was ne'er so thrall'd
But it reserv'd some quantity of choice
To serve in such a difference.] What devil was't
That thus hath cozen'd you at hoodman-blind?
[Eyes without feeling, feeling without sight,
Ears without hands, or eyes, smelling, sans all,
Or but a sickly part of one true sense
Could not so mope.]
O Shame! where is thy blush? Rebellious Hell,
If thou canst mutine in a matron's bones,
To flaming youth, let virtue be as wax,
And melt in her own fire. Proclaim no shame,
When the compulsive ardour gives the charge,
Since frost itself, as actively doth burn
As Reason pandars Will.
QUEEN: O Hamlet, speak no more
Thou turn'st mine eyes into my very soul,
And there I see such black and grained spots,
As will not leave their tinct.
HAMLET: Nay, but to live,
In the rank sweat of an enseamed bed,
Stew'd in corruption; honeying and making love
Over the nasty sty.
QUEEN: O speak to me no more,
These words like daggers enter in mine ears.
No more sweet Hamlet.
HAMLET: A murderer, and a villain:
A slave, that is not twentieth part the tithe
Of your precedent Lord. A vice of Kings,
A cutpurse of the Empire and the rule,

That from a shelf, the precious diadem stole,
And put it in his pocket.

QUEEN: No more.

Enter Ghost.

HAMLET: A King of shreds and patches.
Save me; and hover o'er me with your wings
You heavenly guards. What would your gracious figure?

QUEEN: Alas he's mad.

HAMLET: Do you not come your tardy son to chide,
That laps'd in time and passion, lets go by
Th' important acting of your dread command?
Oh say.

GHOST: Do not forget: this visitation
Is but to whet thy almost blunted purpose.
But look, amazement on thy mother sits;
O step between her, and her fighting soul,
Conceit in weakest bodies, strongest works.
Speak to her Hamlet.

HAMLET: How is it with you Lady?

QUEEN: Alas, how is't with you?
That you bend your eye on vacancy,
And with the incorporal air do hold discourse.
Forth at your eyes your spirits wildly peep,
And as the sleeping soldiers in th' alarm,
Your bedded hair, like life in excrements,
Start up, and stand an end. Oh gentle son,
Upon the heat and flame of thy distemper
Sprinkle cool patience. Whereon do you look?

HAMLET: On him, on him: look you how pale he glares,
His form and cause conjoin'd, preaching to stones,
Would make them capable. Do not look upon me,
Lest with this piteous action you convert
My stern effects: then what I have to do,

Will want true colour; tears perchance for blood.

QUEEN: To whom do you speak this?

HAMLET: Do you see nothing there?

QUEEN: Nothing at all, yet all that is I see.

HAMLET: Nor did you nothing hear?

QUEEN: No, nothing but ourselves.

HAMLET: Why look you there: look how it steals away:
  My father in his habit, as he lived,
    Look where he goes even now out at the portal.

Exit Ghost.

QUEEN: This is the very coinage of your brain,
   This bodiless creation ecstasy
  Is very cunning in.

HAMLET: Ecstasy?
  My pulse as yours doth temperately keep time,
  And makes as healthful music. It is not madness
  That I have uttered; bring me to the test
  And I the matter will re-word, which madness
  Would gambol from. Mother, for love of Grace,
  Lay not a flattering unction to your soul,
  That not your trespass, but my madness speaks:
  It will but skin and film the ulcerous place,
  Whilst rank corruption mining all within,
  Infects unseen. Confess yourself to Heaven,
  Repent what's past, avoid what is to come,
  And do not spread the compost on the weeds,
  To make them ranker. Forgive me this my virtue,
  For in the fatness of these pursy times,
  Virtue itself, of Vice must pardon beg,
  Yea curb, and woo, for leave to do him good.

QUEEN: Oh Hamlet, Thou hast cleft my heart in twain.

HAMLET: O throw away the worser part of it,
  And live the purer with the other half.

Good night, but go not to my uncle's bed,
Assume a virtue, if you have it not,
[That monster custom, who all sense doth eat
Of habits devil, is angel yet in this,
That to the use of actions fair and good,
He likewise gives a frock or livery
That aptly is put on.] Refrain to-night;
And that shall lend a kind of easiness
To the next abstinence. [The next more easy;
For use almost can change the stamp of nature,
And either the devil, or throw him out
With wondrous potency.] Once more good night,
And when you are desirous to be blest,
I'll blessing beg of you. For this same Lord,
I do repent: but Heaven hath pleas'd it so,
To punish me with this, and this with me,
That I must be their scourge and minister.
I will bestow him, and will answer well
The death I gave him: so again, good night.
I must be cruel, only to be kind;
Thus bad begins and worse remains behind.
[One word more good lady.]

QUEEN: What shall I do?

HAMLET: Not this by no means that I bid you do:
Let the bloat King tempt you again to bed,
Pinch wanton on your cheek, call you his mouse,
And let him for a pair of reechy kisses,
Or paddling in your neck with his damn'd fingers,
Make you to ravel all this matter out,
That I essentially am not in madness,
But mad in craft. 'Twere good you let him know,
For who that's but a Queen, fair, sober, wise,
Would from a paddock, from a bat, a gib,

Such dear concernings hide? who would do so?
No, in despite of sense and secrecy,
Unpeg the basket on the house's top,
Let the birds fly, and like the famous ape
To try conclusions in the basket, creep
And break your own neck down.

QUEEN: Be thou assur'd, if words be made of breath,
And breath of life: I have no life to breathe
What thou hast said to me.

HAMLET: I must to England, you know that?

QUEEN: Alack
I had forgot: 'tis so concluded on.

HAMLET: [There's letters seal'd, and my two school-
fellows,
Whom I will trust as I will adders fang'd,
They bear the mandate, they must sweep my way
And marshal me to knavery: let it work,
For 'tis the sport to have the enginer
Hoist with his own petar, and 't shall go hard
But I will delve one yard below their mines,
And blow them at the moon: O 'tis most sweet
When in one line two crafts directly meet.]
This man shall set me packing:
I'll lug the guts into the neighbour room;
Mother good night. Indeed this Councillor
Is now most still, most secret, and most grave,
Who was in life, a foolish prating knave.
Come sir, to draw toward an end with you.
Good night, mother.

    Exit Hamlet tugging in Polonius.

IV. 1

Enter King.

KING: There's matter in these sighs. These profound heaves
  You must translate; 'tis fit we understand them.
  Where is your son?
QUEEN: Ah mine own Lord, what have I seen to-night!
KING: What Gertrude? How does Hamlet?
QUEEN: Mad as the seas, and wind, when both contend
  Which is the mightier: in his lawless fit
  Behind the arras, hearing something stir,
  He whips out his rapier, and cries A rat, a rat,
  And in this brainish apprehension kills
  The unseen good old man.
KING: O heavy deed:
  It had been so with us had we been there:
  His liberty is full of threats to all,
  To you yourself, to us, to every one.
  Alas, how shall this bloody deed be answer'd?
  It will be laid to us, whose providence
  Should have kept short, restrain'd, and out of haunt
  This mad young man. But so much was our love,
  We would not understand what was most fit,
  But like the owner of a foul disease,
  To keep it from divulging, lets it feed
  Even on the pith of life. Where is he gone?
QUEEN: To draw apart the body he hath kill'd,
  O'er whom his very madness like some ore
  Among a mineral of metals base
  Shows itself pure. He weeps for what is done.
KING: O Gertrude, come away:

The sun no sooner shall the mountains touch,
But we will ship him hence, and this vile deed,
We must with all our majesty and skill
Both countenance, and excuse. Ho Guildenstern:
   Enter Rosencrantz and Guildenstern.
Friends both go join you with some further aid:
Hamlet in madness hath Polonius slain,
And from his mother's closet hath he dragg'd him.
Go seek him out, speak fair, and bring the body
Into the Chapel. I pray you haste in this.
   Exeunt Rosencrantz and Guildenstern.
Come Gertrude, we'll call up our wisest friends,
To let them know both what we mean to do,
And what's untimely done
[Whose whisper o'er the world's diameter,
As level as the cannon to his blank,
Transports his poison'd shot, may miss our name,
And hit the woundless air]. O come away.
My soul is full of discord and dismay.
   Exeunt.

IV.2

Enter Hamlet.

HAMLET: Safely stowed.

ROSENCRANTZ
GUILDENSTERN } [*Within*] Hamlet, Lord Hamlet.

HAMLET: What noise? Who calls on Hamlet? O here they
 come.

   Enter Rosencrantz and Guildenstern.

ROSENCRANTZ: What have you done my Lord with the
 dead body?

HAMLET: Compounded it with dust, whereto 'tis kin.

ROSENCRANTZ: Tell us where 'tis, that we may take it
thence,
And bear it to the Chapel.

HAMLET: Do not believe it.

ROSENCRANTZ: Believe what?

HAMLET: That I can keep your counsel, and not mine
own. Besides, to be demanded of a sponge, what replication should be made by the son of a King?

ROSENCRANTZ: Take you me for a sponge, my Lord?

HAMLET: Ay sir, that soaks up the King's countenance, his
rewards, his authorities. But such officers do the King
best service in the end. He keeps them like an ape in the
corner of his jaw, first mouth'd to be last swallowed,
when he needs what you have glean'd, it is but squeezing
you, and sponge you shall be dry again.

ROSENCRANTZ: I understand you not my Lord.

HAMLET: I am glad of it: a knavish speech sleeps in a
foolish ear.

ROSENCRANTZ: My Lord, you must tell us where the
body is, and go with us to the King.

HAMLET: The body is with the King, but the King is not
with the body. The King is a thing –

GUILDENSTERN: A thing my Lord?

HAMLET: Of nothing: bring me to him, hide fox, and all
after.

Exeunt.

IV.3

Enter King.

KING: I have sent to seek him, and to find the body:
How dangerous is it that this man goes loose:
Yet must not we put the strong Law on him:

He's loved of the distracted multitude,
Who like not in their judgement, but their eyes:
And where 'tis so, th' offender's scourge is weigh'd
But never the offence: to bear all smooth, and even,
This sudden sending him away, must seem
Deliberate pause; diseases desperate grown,
By desperate appliance are relieved,
Or not at all.

Enter Rosencrantz.

How now? what hath befall'n?

ROSENCRANTZ: Where the dead body is bestow'd my
  Lord,
We cannot get from him.

KING: But where is he?

ROSENCRANTZ: Without my Lord, guarded to know your
  pleasure.

KING: Bring him before us.

ROSENCRANTZ: Hoa, Guildenstern! Bring in my Lord.

Enter Hamlet and Guildenstern.

KING: Now Hamlet, where's Polonius?

HAMLET: At supper.

KING: At supper? Where?

HAMLET: Not where he eats, but where he is eaten, a certain convocation of politic worms are e'en at him. Your
  worm is your only Emperor for diet. We fat all creatures
  else to fat us, and we fat ourselves for maggots. Your fat
  King and your lean beggar, is but variable service, two
  dishes but to one table; that's the end.

[KING: Alas, alas.

HAMLET: A man may fish with the worm that hath eat
  of a King, and eat of the fish that hath fed of that
  worm.]

KING: What dost thou mean by this?

HAMLET: Nothing but to show you how a King may go
a progress through the guts of a beggar.

KING: Where is Polonius?

HAMLET: In heaven, send hither to see. If your messenger
find him not there, seek him i' th' other place yourself:
but indeed, if you find him not within this month, you
shall nose him as you go up the stairs into the lobby.

KING: Go seek him there.

HAMLET: He will stay till ye come.

KING: Hamlet, this deed for thine especial safety,
Which we do tender, as we dearly grieve
For that which thou hast done, must send thee hence
With fiery quickness. Therefore prepare thyself,
The bark is ready, and the wind at help,
Th' associates tend, and every thing is bent
For England.

HAMLET: For England?

KING: Ay Hamlet.

HAMLET: Good.

KING: So is it, if thou knew'st our purposes.

HAMLET: I see a cherub that sees them: but come, for
England. Farewell dear mother.

KING: Thy loving father Hamlet.

HAMLET: My mother: father and mother is man and wife;
man and wife is one flesh, and so my mother. Come, for
England.

Exit.

KING: Follow him at foot, tempt him with speed aboard:
Delay it not, I'll have him hence to-night.
Away, for every thing is seal'd and done
That else leans on th' affair; pray you make haste.
And England, if my love thou hold'st at aught,
As my great power thereof may give thee sense,

Since yet thy cicatrice looks raw and red
After the Danish sword, and thy free awe
Pays homage to us; thou mayst not coldly set
Our sovereign process, which imports at full
By letters conjuring to that effect
The present death of Hamlet. Do it England,
For like the hectic in my blood he rages,
And thou must cure me; till I know 'tis done,
Howe'er my haps, my joys were ne'er begun.

Exit.

IV. 4

Enter Fortinbras with his army over the stage.

FORTINBRAS: Go Captain, from me greet the Danish
   King,
Tell him, that by his license Fortinbras
Craves the conveyance of a promis'd march
Over his Kingdom. You know the rendezvous:
If that his Majesty would aught with us,
We shall express our duty in his eye,
And let him know so.
CAPTAIN: I will do't my Lord.
FORTINBRAS: Go softly on.

Exeunt Fortinbras and Soldiers.

[*Enter Hamlet, Rosencrantz, and others.*

HAMLET: Good sir whose powers are these?
CAPTAIN: They are of Norway sir.
HAMLET: How purpos'd sir I pray you?
CAPTAIN: Against some part of Poland.
HAMLET: Who commands them sir?
CAPTAIN: The nephew to old Norway, Fortinbras.
HAMLET: Goes it against the main of Poland sir,

Or for some frontier?

CAPTAIN: Truly to speak, and with no addition,
We go to gain a little patch of ground
That hath in it no profit but the name:
To pay five ducats, five I would not farm it;
Nor will it yield to Norway or the Pole
A ranker rate, should it be sold in fee.

HAMLET: Why then the Polack never will defend it.

CAPTAIN: Yes, it is already garrison'd.

HAMLET: Two thousand souls, and twenty thousand ducats
Will not debate the question of this straw.
This is th' imposthume of much wealth and peace,
That inward breaks, and shows no cause without
Why the man dies. I humbly thank you sir.

CAPTAIN: God buy you, sir.

Exit.

ROSENCRANTZ: Will't please you go my Lord?

HAMLET: I'll be with you straight, go a little before.

Exeunt all but Hamlet.

How all occasions do inform against me,
And spur my dull revenge. What is a man
If his chief good and market of his time
Be but to sleep and feed? a beast, no more:
Sure he that made us with such large discourse
Looking before and after, gave us not
That capability and god-like reason
To fust in us unus'd. Now whether it be
Bestial oblivion, or some craven scruple
Of thinking too precisely on th' event,
A thought which quarter'd hath but one part wisdom,
And ever three parts coward, I do not know
Why yet I live to say This thing's to do,

Sith I have cause, and will, and strength, and means
To do't; examples gross as earth exhort me,
Witness this army of such mass and charge,
Led by a delicate and tender Prince,
Whose spirit with divine ambition puff'd,
Makes mouths at the invisible event,
Exposing what is mortal, and unsure,
To all that fortune, death, and danger dare,
Even for an egg-shell. Rightly to be great,
Is not to stir without great argument,
But greatly to find quarrel in a straw
When honour's at the stake. How stand I then
That have a father kill'd, a mother stain'd,
Excitements of my reason, and my blood,
And let all sleep, while to my shame I see
The imminent death of twenty thousand men,
That for a fantasy and trick of fame
Go to their graves like beds, fight for a plot
Whereon the numbers cannot try the cause,
Which is not tomb enough and continent
To hide the slain? O from this time forth,
My thoughts be bloody, or be nothing worth.]
                    Exit.

IV.5

Enter Queen and Horatio.

QUEEN: I will not speak with her.
HORATIO: She is importunate, indeed distract,
  Her mood will needs be pitied.
QUEEN: What would she have?
HORATIO: She speaks much of her father; says she hears
  There's tricks i' th' world, and hems, and beats her heart,

Spurns enviously at straws, speaks things in doubt,
That carry but half sense; her speech is nothing,
Yet the unshaped use of it doth move
The hearers to collection; they aim at it,
And botch the words up fit to their own thoughts,
Which as her winks, and nods, and gestures yield them,
Indeed would make one think there might be thought,
Though nothing sure, yet much unhappily.

QUEEN: 'Twere good she were spoken with, for she may strew
Dangerous conjectures in ill-breeding minds.
Let her come in.
To my sick soul (as sin's true nature is)
Each toy seems prologue, to some great amiss:
So full of artless jealousy is guilt,
It spills itself, in fearing to be spilt.

Enter Ophelia, distracted.

OPHELIA: Where is the beauteous Majesty of Denmark?
QUEEN: How now Ophelia?
OPHELIA:

She Sings.

> *How should I your true love know*
> *From another one?*
> *By his cockle hat and staff,*
> *And his sandal shoon.*

QUEEN: Alas sweet Lady: what imports this song?
OPHELIA: Say you? nay pray you mark.

> *He is dead and gone Lady,*
> *He is dead and gone,*
> *At his head a grass-green turf,*
> *At his heels a stone.*

Enter King.

QUEEN: Nay but Ophelia.

OPHELIA: Pray you mark.
>   *White his shroud as the mountain snow.*

QUEEN: Alas, look here my Lord.

OPHELIA:
>   *Larded with sweet flowers:*
>   *Which bewept to the grave did not go*
>   *With true-love showers.*

KING: How do ye, pretty Lady?

OPHELIA: Well, God 'ild you. They say the owl was a baker's daughter. Lord, we know what we are, but know not what we may be. God be at your table.

KING: Conceit upon her father.

OPHELIA: Pray you let's have no words of this: but when they ask you what it means, say you this:
>   *To-morrow is Saint Valentine's day,*
>   *All in the morning betime,*
>   *And I a maid at your window,*
>   *To be your Valentine.*
>   *Then up he rose, and donn'd his clothes,*
>   *And dupped the chamber door,*
>   *Let in the maid, that out a maid*
>   *Never departed more.*

KING: Pretty Ophelia.

OPHELIA: Indeed la, without an oath I'll make an end on't
>   *By Gis, and by Saint Charity,*
>   *Alack, and fie for shame:*
>   *Young men will do't, if they come to 't,*
>   *By Cock they are to blame.*
>   *Quoth she, before you tumbled me,*
>   *You promis'd me to wed.*
>   *So would I ha' done by yonder sun,*
>   *And thou hadst not come to my bed.*

KING: How long hath she been thus?

OPHELIA: I hope all will be well. We must be patient, but
I cannot choose but weep, to think they should lay him
i' th' cold ground: my brother shall know of it, and so I
thank you for your good counsel. Come, my coach:
good night Ladies: good night sweet Ladies: good night,
good night.

Exit.

KING: Follow her close, give her good watch I pray you:
Exit Horatio.

O this is the poison of deep grief, it springs
All from her father's death. O Gertrude, Gertrude,
When sorrows come, they come not single spies,
But in battalions. First, her father slain,
Next your son gone, and he most violent author
Of his own just remove: the people muddied,
Thick and unwholesome in their thoughts, and whispers
For good Polonius' death; and we have done but greenly
In hugger-mugger to inter him. Poor Ophelia
Divided from herself, and her fair judgement,
Without the which we are pictures, or mere beasts.
Last, and as much containing as all these,
Her brother is in secret come from France,
Feeds on his wonder, keeps himself in clouds,
And wants not buzzers to infect his ear
With pestilent speeches of his father's death,
Wherein necessity of matter beggar'd,
Will nothing stick our persons to arraign
In ear and ear. O my dear Gertrude, this,
Like to a murdering-piece in many places,
Gives me superfluous death.

A noise within. Enter a Messenger.

QUEEN: Alack, what noise is this?
KING: Where are my Switzers? Let them guard the door.

What is the matter?

MESSENGER: Save yourself, my Lord.
The ocean (overpeering of his list)
Eats not the flats with more impiteous haste
Than young Laertes, in a riotous head,
O'erbears your officers, the rabble call him Lord,
And as the world were now but to begin,
Antiquity forgot, custom not known,
The ratifiers and props of every word,
They cry Choose we! Laertes shall be King,
Caps, hands, and tongues, applaud it to the clouds,
Laertes shall be King, Laertes King.

QUEEN: How cheerfully on the false trail they cry.
O this is counter you false Danish dogs.

Noise within.

KING: The doors are broke.

Enter Laertes with others.

LAERTES: Where is this King, sirs? stand you all without.

ALL: No, let's come in.

LAERTES: I pray you give me leave.

ALL: We will, we will.

Exeunt.

LAERTES: I thank you: keep the door. O thou vile King,
Give me my father.

QUEEN: Calmly good Laertes.

LAERTES: That drop of blood that's calm proclaims me
bastard,
Cries cuckold to my father, brands the harlot
Even here, between the chaste unsmirched brow
Of my true mother.

KING: What is the cause Laertes,
That thy rebellion looks so giant-like?
Let him go Gertrude: do not fear our person:

There's such divinity doth hedge a King,
That Treason can but peep to what it would,
Acts little of his will. Tell me Laertes,
Why thou art thus incensed? Let him go Gertrude.
Speak man.

LAERTES: Where is my father?

KING: Dead.

QUEEN: But not by him.

KING: Let him demand his fill.

LAERTES: How came he dead? I'll not be juggl'd with.
To hell allegiance: vows, to the blackest devil.
Conscience and grace, to the profoundest pit.
I dare damnation: to this point I stand,
That both the worlds I give to negligence,
Let come what comes: only I'll be reveng'd
Most throughly for my father.

KING: Who shall stay you?

LAERTES: My will, not all the world;
And for my means, I'll husband them so well,
They shall go far with little.

KING: Good Laertes:
If you desire to know the certainty
Of your dear father's death, is't writ in your revenge,
That swoopstake you will draw both friend and foe,
Winner and loser?

LAERTES: None but his enemies.

KING: Will you know them then?

LAERTES: To his good friends, thus wide I'll ope my arms:
And like the kind life-rendering pelican,
Repast them with my blood.

KING: Why now you speak
Like a good child, and a true gentleman.
That I am guiltless of your father's death,

And am most sensibly in grief for it,
It shall as level to your judgement pierce
As day does to your eye.

A noise within: 'Let her come in.'
Enter Ophelia.

LAERTES: How now? what noise is that?
O heat dry up my brains, tears seven times salt,
Burn out the sense and virtue of mine eye.
By Heaven, thy madness shall be paid by weight,
Till our scale turns the beam. O Rose of May,
Dear maid, kind sister, sweet Ophelia:
O Heavens, is't possible a young maid's wits
Should be as mortal as an old man's life?
Nature is fine in love, and where 'tis fine,
It sends some precious instance of itself
After the thing it loves.

OPHELIA: *Sings.*
> *They bore him barefac'd on the bier,*
> *Hey non nonny, nonny, hey nonny;*
> *And on his grave rain'd many a tear,*

Fare you well my dove.

LAERTES: Hadst thou thy wits, and didst persuade revenge,
It could not move thus.

OPHELIA: You must sing down a-down,
An you call him a-down-a.
Oh, how the wheel becomes it! It is the false steward
that stole his master's daughter.

LAERTES: This nothing's more than matter.

OPHELIA: There's rosemary, that's for remembrance.
Pray love remember: and there is pansies, that's for
thoughts.

LAERTES: A document in madness, thoughts and remembrance fitted.

OPHELIA: There's fennel for you, and columbines: there's
rue for you, and here's some for me. We may call it herb
of grace a' Sundays: Oh you must wear your rue with
a difference. There's a daisy, I would give you some violets, but they wither'd all when my father died: they
say, he made a good end;

> *For bonny sweet Robin is all my joy.*

LAERTES: Thought, and affliction, passion, hell itself,
She turns to favour, and to prettiness.

OPHELIA: *And will he not come again,*
> *And will he not come again?*
>> *No, no, he is dead,*
>> *Go to thy death-bed,*
> *He never will come again,*
> *His bear was as white as snow,*
> *All flaxen was his poll:*
>> *He is gone, he is gone,*
>> *And we cast away moan,*
> *Gramercy on his soul,*

And of all Christian souls, I pray God. God buy ye.

> *Exit Ophelia.*

LAERTES: Do you see this, O God?

KING: Laertes, I must commune with your grief,
Or you deny me right: go but apart,
Make choice of whom your wisest friends you will,
And they shall hear and judge 'twixt you and me;
If by direct or by collateral hand
They find us touch'd, we will our Kingdom give,
Our Crown, our life, and all that we call ours
To you in satisfaction. But if not,
Be you content to lend your patience to us,
And we shall jointly labour with your soul
To give it due content.

LAERTES: Let this be so:
  His means of death, his obscure burial,
  No trophy, sword, nor hatchment o'er his bones,
  No noble rite, nor formal ostentation,
  Cry to be heard, as 'twere from Heaven to Earth,
  That I must call in question.

KING: So you shall:
  And where th' offence is, let the great axe fall.
  I pray you go with me.

Exeunt.

IV.6

Enter Horatio, with an Attendant.

HORATIO: What are they that would speak with me?

ATTENDANT: Sailors, sir, they say they have letters for you.

HORATIO: Let them come in,
  I do not know from what part of the world
  I should be greeted, if not from Lord Hamlet.

Enter Sailor.

SAILOR: God bless you sir.

HORATIO: Let him bless thee too.

SAILOR: He shall sir, and please him. There's a letter for
  you sir: it comes from th' ambassadors that was bound
  for England, if your name be Horatio, as I am let to
  know it is.

HORATIO reads the letter: *Horatio, when thou shalt have
  o'erlooked this, give these fellows some means to the King;
  they have letters for him. Ere we were two days old at sea, a
  pirate of very warlike appointment gave us chase. Finding
  ourselves too slow of sail, we put on a compelled valour. In
  the grapple, I boarded them: on the instant they got clear of
  our ship, so I alone became their prisoner. They have dealt*

*with me, like thieves of mercy, but they knew what they did.
I am to do a good turn for them. Let the King have the letters
I have sent, and repair thou to me with as much haste as thou
wouldst fly death. I have words to speak in your ear, will
make thee dumb, yet are they much too light for the bore of the
matter. These good fellows will bring thee where I am.
Rosencrantz and Guildenstern hold their course for England.
Of them I have much to tell thee, farewell. He that thou
knowest thine,* HAMLET.

Come, I will give way for these your letters,
And do't the speedier, that you may direct me
To him from whom you brought them.

Exeunt.

IV.7

Enter King and Laertes.

KING: Now must your conscience my acquittance seal,
    And you must put me in your heart for friend,
    Sith you have heard, and with a knowing ear,
    That he which hath your noble father slain,
    Pursued my life.

LAERTES: It well appears. But tell me,
    Why you proceeded not against these feats,
    So crimeful, and so capital in nature,
    As by your safety, wisdom, all things else,
    You mainly were stirr'd up.

KING: O for two special reasons,
    Which may to you (perhaps) seem much unsinew'd,
    And yet to me they are strong. The Queen his mother,
    Lives almost by his looks: and for myself,
    My virtue or my plague, be it either which,
    She's so conjunctive to my life and soul,

That as the star moves not but in his sphere,
I could not but by her. The other motive,
Why to a public count I might not go,
Is the great love the general gender bear him,
Who dipping all his faults in their affection,
Would like the spring that turneth wood to stone,
Convert his gyves to graces. So that my arrows
Too slightly timber'd for so loud a wind,
Would have reverted to my bow again,
And not where I had aim'd them.

LAERTES: And so have I a noble father lost,
A sister driven into desperate terms,
Whose worth (if praises may go back again)
Stood challenger on mount of all the age
For her perfections. But my revenge will come.

KING: Break not your sleeps for that, you must not think
That we are made of stuff, so flat, and dull,
That we can let our beard be shook with danger,
And think it pastime. You shortly shall hear more,
I lov'd your father, and we love ourself,
And that I hope will teach you to imagine—

Enter a Messenger.

How now? What news?

MESSENGER: Letters my Lord from Hamlet.
This to your Majesty: this to the Queen.

KING: From Hamlet? Who brought them?

MESSENGER: Sailors my Lord they say, I saw them not:
They were given to me by Claudio, he receiv'd them
Of him that brought them.

KING: Laertes you shall hear them:
Leave us.

Exit Messenger.

High and Mighty, You shall know I am set naked on your

*Kingdom. To-morrow shall I beg leave to see your kingly
eyes. When I shall (first asking your pardon thereunto) re-
count the occasions of my sudden and more strange return.*

HAMLET

What should this mean? Are all the rest come back?
Or is it some abuse? or no such thing?

LAERTES: Know you the hand?

KING: 'Tis Hamlet's character. Naked,
And in a postscript here he says alone:
Can you advise me?

LAERTES: I'm lost in it my Lord; but let him come,
It warms the very sickness in my heart,
That I shall live and tell him to his teeth;
Thus didest thou.

KING: If it be so Laertes,
As how should it be so, how otherwise,
Will you be rul'd by me?

LAERTES: If so you'll not o'errule me to a peace.

KING: To thine own peace: if he be now return'd,
As checking at his voyage, and that he means
No more to undertake it; I will work him
To an exploit now ripe in my device,
Under the which he shall not choose but fall:
And for his death no wind of blame shall breathe,
But even his mother shall uncharge the practice,
And call it accident.

[LAERTES: My Lord I will be ruled,
The rather if you could devise it so
That I might be the organ.

KING: It falls right,
You have been talk'd of since your travel much,
And that in Hamlet's hearing, for a quality
Wherein they say you shine, your sum of parts

Did not together pluck such envy from him
As did that one, and that in my regard
Of the unworthiest siege.
LAERTES: What part is that my Lord?
KING: A very riband in the cap of youth,
Yet needful too, for youth no less becomes
The light and careless livery that it wears
Than settled age, his sables, and his weeds,
Importing health and graveness.] Some two months hence,
Here was a gentleman of Normandy,
I've seen myself, and serv'd against the French,
And they can well on horseback; but this gallant
Had witchcraft in't; he grew into his seat,
And to such wondrous doing brought his horse,
As he had been incorps'd and demi-natur'd
With the brave beast, so far he pass'd my thought,
That I in forgery of shapes and tricks,
Come short of what he did.
LAERTES: A Norman was't?
KING: A Norman.
LAERTES: Upon my life Lamound.
KING: The very same.
LAERTES: I know him well, he is the brooch indeed,
And gem of all the nation.
KING: He made confession of you,
And gave you such a masterly report,
For art and exercise in your defence;
And for your rapier most especially,
That he cried out, 'twould be a sight indeed,
If one could match you [the scrimers of their nation
He swore had neither motion, guard nor eye,
If you oppos'd them;] sir, this report of his
Did Hamlet so envenom with his envy,

That he could nothing do but wish and beg,
Your sudden coming o'er to play with him;
Now out of this.

LAERTES: What out of this, my Lord?

KING: Laertes was your father dear to you?
Or are you like the painting of a sorrow,
A face without a heart?

LAERTES: Why ask you this?

KING: Not that I think you did not love your father,
But that I know Love is begun by Time:
And that I see in passages of proof,
Time qualifies the spark and fire of it:
[There lives within the very flame of love
A kind of wick or snuff that will abate it,
And nothing is at a like goodness still,
For goodness growing to a plurisy,
Dies in his own too much; that we would do.
We should do when we would: for this would changes
And hath abatements and delays as many,
As there are tongues, are hands, are accidents,
And then this should is like a spendthrift's sigh,
That hurts by easing; but, to the quick of th' ulcer,]
Hamlet comes back: what would you undertake,
To show yourself your father's son indeed,
More than in words?

LAERTES: To cut his throat i' th' Church.

KING: No place indeed should murder sanctuarize;
Revenge should have no bounds: but good Laertes
Will you do this, keep close within your chamber,
Hamlet return'd, shall know you are come home:
We'll put on those shall praise your excellence,
And set a double varnish on the fame
The Frenchman gave you, bring you in fine together,

And wager on your heads; he being remiss,
Most generous, and free from all contriving,
Will not peruse the foils! so that with ease,
Or with a little shuffling, you may choose
A sword unbated, and in a pass of practice,
Requite him for your father.

LAERTES: I will do't,
And for that purpose I'll anoint my sword:
I bought an unction of a mountebank
So mortal, that but dip a knife in it,
Where it draws blood, no cataplasm so rare,
Collected from all simples that have virtue
Under the Moon, can save the thing from death,
That is but scratch'd withal: I'll touch my point,
With this contagion, that if I gall him slightly,
It may be death.

KING: Let's further think of this,
Weigh what convenience both of time and means
May fit us to our shape, if this should fail;
And that our drift look through our bad performance,
'Twere better not assay'd; therefore this project
Should have a back or second, that might hold,
If this should blast in proof: soft, let me see,
We'll make a solemn wager on your cunnings,
I ha't:
When in your motion you are hot and dry,
As make your bouts more violent to that end,
And that he calls for drink; I'll have prepar'd him
A chalice for the nonce; whereon but sipping,
If he by chance escape your venom'd stuck,
Our purpose may hold there;
How sweet Queen.

Enter Queen.

QUEEN: One woe doth tread upon another's heel,
So fast they follow: your sister's drown'd, Laertes.

LAERTES: Drown'd! O where?

QUEEN: There is a willow grows aslant a brook,
That shows his hoar leaves in the glassy stream:
There with fantastic garlands did she come,
Of crow-flowers, nettles, daisies, and long purples,
That liberal shepherds give a grosser name;
But our cold maids do dead men's fingers call them:
There on the pendent boughs, her coronet weeds
Clambering to hang; an envious sliver broke,
When down her weedy trophies, and herself
Fell in the weeping brook; her clothes spread wide,
And mermaid-like, awhile they bore her up,
Which time she chanted snatches of old tunes,
As one incapable of her own distress,
Or like a creature native, and indued
Unto that element: but long it could not be,
Till that her garments, heavy with their drink,
Pull'd the poor wretch from her melodious lay,
To muddy death.

LAERTES: Alas then, she is drown'd?

QUEEN: Drown'd, drown'd.

LAERTES: Too much of water hast thou poor Ophelia,
And therefore I forbid my tears: but yet
It is our trick, Nature her custom holds,
Let shame say what it will; when these are gone.
The woman will be out: adieu my Lord,
I have a speech of fire, that fain would blaze,
But that this folly douts it.

Exit.

KING: Let's follow, Gertrude:
How much I had to do to calm his rage!

Now fear I this will give it start again;
Therefore let's follow.

Exeunt.

V.I

Enter two Clowns.

FIRST CLOWN: Is she to be buried in Christian burial, that
  wilfully seeks her own salvation?

SECOND CLOWN: I tell thee she is, and therefore make her
  grave straight, the crowner hath sat on her, and finds it
  Christian burial.

FIRST CLOWN: How can that be, unless she drowned herself in her own defence?

SECOND CLOWN: Why, 'tis found so.

FIRST CLOWN: It must be *se offendendo*, it cannot be else:
  for here lies the point; if I drown myself wittingly, it
  argues an act: and an act hath three branches; it is to act,
  to do, and to perform; argal she drown'd herself
  wittingly.

SECOND CLOWN: Nay but hear you goodman delver.

FIRST CLOWN: Give me leave; here lies the water; good:
  here stands the man; good: if the man go to this water
  and drown himself; it is will he nill he, he goes; mark
  you that? but if the water come to him and drown him,
  he drowns not himself. Argal, he that is not guilty of his
  own death, shortens not his own life.

SECOND CLOWN: But is this law?

FIRST CLOWN: Ay marry is't, crowner's Quest Law.

SECOND CLOWN: Will you ha' the truth on't: if this had
  not been a gentlewoman, she should have been buried
  out of Christian burial.

FIRST CLOWN: Why there thou say'st. And the more pity

that great folk should have countenance in this world to drown or hang themselves, more than their even Christian. Come, my spade; there is no ancient gentlemen, but gardeners, ditchers and grave-makers; they hold up Adam's profession.

SECOND CLOWN: Was he a gentleman?

FIRST CLOWN: He was the first that ever bore arms.

SECOND CLOWN: Why he had none.

FIRST CLOWN: What, art a heathen? How dost thou understand the Scripture? The Scripture says Adam digg'd; could he dig without arms? I'll put another question to thee; if thou answerest me not to the purpose, confess thyself —

SECOND CLOWN: Go to.

FIRST CLOWN: What is he that builds stronger than either the mason, the shipwright, or the carpenter?

SECOND CLOWN: The gallows-maker; for that frame outlives a thousand tenants.

FIRST CLOWN: I like thy wit well in good faith, the gallows does well; but how does it well? it does well to those that do ill: now, thou dost ill to say the gallows is built stronger than the church: argal, the gallows may do well to thee. To't again, come.

SECOND CLOWN: Who builds stronger than a mason, a shipwright, or a carpenter?

FIRST CLOWN: Ay, tell me that, and unyoke.

SECOND CLOWN: Marry, now I can tell.

FIRST CLOWN: To't.

SECOND CLOWN: Mass, I cannot tell.

Enter Hamlet and Horatio afar off.

FIRST CLOWN: Cudgel thy brains no more about it; for your dull ass will not mend his pace with beating; and when you are ask'd this question next, say a grave-maker: the

houses that he makes, last till Doomsday: go, get thee
to Yaughan, fetch me a stoup of liquor.

Exit Second Clown.

    Sings

        In youth when I did love, did love
        Methought it was very sweet:
        To contract O the time for a my behove,
        O methought there was nothing meet.

HAMLET: Has this fellow no feelings of his business, that he
sings at grave-making?

HORATIO: Custom hath made it in him a property of
easiness.

HAMLET: 'Tis e'en so; the hand of little employment hath
the daintier sense.

FIRST CLOWN: *Sings*

        But Age with his stealing steps
        Hath claw'd me in his clutch:
        And hath shipped me intil the land,
        As if I had never been such.

HAMLET: That skull had a tongue in it, and could sing
once: how the knave jowls it to th' ground, as if it were
Cain's jaw-bone, that did the first murther: it might be
the pate of a politician which this ass now o'er-reaches:
one that would circumvent God, might it not?

HORATIO: It might, my Lord.

HAMLET: Or of a courtier, which could say, Good-
morrow sweet Lord: how dost thou, good Lord? This
might be my Lord such-a-one, that prais'd my Lord such-
a-one's horse, when he meant to beg it; might it not?

HORATIO: Ay, my Lord.

HAMLET: Why e'en so: and now my Lady Worm's, chapless, and knocked about the mazzard with a sexton's
spade; here's fine revolution, if we had the trick to see't.

Did these bones cost no more the breeding, but to play
at loggats with 'em? mine ache to think on't.

FIRST CLOWN: *Sings*

> *A pick-haxe and a spade, a spade,*
> *For and a shrouding sheet:*
> *O a pit of clay for to be made,*
> *For such a guest is meet.*

HAMLET: There's another: why might not that be the
skull of a lawyer? Where be his quiddits now? his
quillets? his cases? his tenures, and his tricks? why does
he suffer this rude knave now to knock him about the
sconce with a dirty shovel, and will not tell him of his
action of battery? Hum. This fellow might be in's time
a great buyer of land, with his statutes, his recognizances,
his fines, his double vouchers, his recoveries: is this the
fine of his fines, and the recovery of his recoveries, to
have his fine pate full of fine dirt? will his vouchers
vouch him no more of his purchases, and double ones
too, than the length and breadth of a pair of indentures?
The very conveyances of his lands will hardly lie in this
box; and must the inheritor himself have no more? ha?

HORATIO: Not a jot more my Lord.

HAMLET: Is not parchment made of sheep-skins?

HORATIO: Ay my Lord, and of calf-skins too.

HAMLET: They are sheep and calves that seek out assurance in that. I will speak to this fellow: whose grave's
this sir?

FIRST CLOWN: Mine sir:

> *O a pit of clay for to be made,*
> *For such a guest is meet.*

HAMLET: I think it be thine indeed: for thou liest in't.

FIRST CLOWN: You lie out on't sir, and therefore 'tis not
yours: for my part, I do not lie in't; and yet it is mine.

HAMLET: Thou dost lie in't to be in't and say it is thine:
'tis for the dead, not for the quick, therefore thou liest.

FIRST CLOWN: 'Tis a quick lie sir, 'twill away again from
me to you.

HAMLET: What man dost thou dig it for?

FIRST CLOWN: For no man sir.

HAMLET: What woman then?

FIRST CLOWN: For none neither.

HAMLET: Who is to be buried in't?

FIRST CLOWN: One that was a woman sir; but rest her
soul, she's dead.

HAMLET: How absolute the knave is! we must speak by
the card, or equivocation will undo us. By the Lord
Horatio, this three years I have taken note of it, the age
is grown so picked, that the toe of the peasant comes so
near the heel of our courtier, he galls his kibe. How long
hast thou been a grave-maker?

FIRST CLOWN: Of all the days i' th' year, I came to't that
day that our last King Hamlet o'ercame Fortinbras.

HAMLET: How long is that since?

FIRST CLOWN: Cannot you tell that? every fool can tell
that: it was the very day that young Hamlet was born,
he that is mad, and sent into England.

HAMLET: Ay marry, why was he sent into England?

FIRST CLOWN: Why, because he was mad; he shall recover his wits there; or if he do not, it's no great matter
there.

HAMLET: Why?

FIRST CLOWN: 'Twill not be seen in him there, there the
men are as mad as he.

HAMLET: How came he mad?

FIRST CLOWN: Very strangely they say.

HAMLET: How strangely?

FIRST CLOWN: Faith e'en with losing his wits.

HAMLET: Upon what ground?

FIRST CLOWN: Why here in Denmark: I have been sexton here, man and boy thirty years.

HAMLET: How long will a man lie i' th' earth ere he rot?

FIRST CLOWN: I' faith, if he be not rotten before he die, (as we have many pocky corses nowadays, that will scarce hold the laying in) he will last you some eight year, or nine year. A tanner will last you nine year.

HAMLET: Why he, more than another?

FIRST CLOWN: Why sir, his hide is so tann'd with his trade, that he will keep out water a great while. And your water, is a sore decayer of your whoreson dead body. Here's a skull now: this skull, has lain in the earth three and twenty years.

HAMLET: Whose was it?

FIRST CLOWN: A whoreson mad fellow's it was; whose do you think it was?

HAMLET: Nay, I know not.

FIRST CLOWN: A pestilence on him for a mad rogue, a' pour'd a flagon of Rhenish on my head once. This same skull sir, this same skull sir, was Yorick's skull, the King's Jester.

HAMLET: This?

FIRST CLOWN: E'en that.

HAMLET: Let me see. Alas poor Yorick, I knew him Horatio, a fellow of infinite jest; of most excellent fancy, he hath borne me on his back a thousand times: and now how abhorred in my imagination it is, my gorge rises at it. Here hung those lips, that I have kiss'd I know not how oft. Where be your gibes now? your gambols? your songs? your flashes of merriment that were wont to set the table on a roar? Not one now to mock your

own jeering? quite chop-fallen? Now get you to my
Lady's chamber, and tell her, let her paint an inch thick,
to this favour she must come. Make her laugh at that:
prithee Horatio tell me one thing.

HORATIO: What's that my Lord?

HAMLET: Dost thou think Alexander look'd o' this fashion
i' th' earth?

HORATIO: E'en so.

HAMLET: And smelt so? puh.

HORATIO: E'en so, my Lord.

HAMLET: To what base uses we may return, Horatio. Why
may not imagination trace the noble dust of Alexander,
till he find it stopping a bung-hole?

HORATIO: 'Twere to consider too curiously, to consider
so.

HAMLET: No faith, not a jot. But to follow him thither
with modesty enough, and likelihood to lead it; as thus.
Alexander died: Alexander was buried: Alexander re-
turneth into dust; the dust is earth; of earth we make
loam, and why of that loam (whereto he was converted)
might they not stop a beer-barrel?

    Imperial Cæsar, dead and turn'd to clay.

    Might stop a hole to keep the wind away.

    O, that that earth, which kept the world in awe,

    Should patch a wall, t' expel the winter's flaw.

But soft, but soft, aside; here comes the King.

*Enter bearers with a Coffin, the King and Queen, Laertes and
other Lords, a Priest following.*

The Queen, the courtiers. Who is that they follow,
And with such maimed rites? This doth betoken,
The corse they follow, did with desperate hand,
Fordo its own life; 'twas of some estate.
Couch we awhile, and mark.

LAERTES: What ceremony else?

HAMLET: That is Laertes, a very noble youth: mark.

LAERTES: What ceremony else?

PRIEST: Her obsequies have been as far enlarg'd.
As we have warrantise, her death was doubtful,
And but that great command o'ersways the order,
She should in ground unsanctified have lodg'd,
Till the last Trumpet. For charitable prayer,
Shards, flints, and pebbles, should be thrown on her:
Yet here she is allow'd her virgin rites,
Her maiden strewments, and the bringing home
Of bell and burial.

LAERTES: Must there no more be done?

PRIEST: No more be done:
We should profane the service of the dead,
To sing sage *requiem*, and such rest to her
As to peace-parted souls.

LAERTES: Lay her i' th' earth,
And from her fair and unpolluted flesh,
May violets spring. I tell thee (churlish priest)
A ministering angel shall my sister be,
When thou liest howling.

HAMLET: What, the fair Ophelia?

QUEEN: Sweets to the sweet, farewell.
I hop'd thou shouldst have been my Hamlet's wife:
I thought thy bride-bed to have deck'd (sweet maid)
And not have strew'd thy grave.

LAERTES: O treble woe,
Fall ten times treble on that cursed head
Whose wicked deed thy most ingenious sense
Depriv'd thee of. Hold off the earth awhile,
Till I have caught her once more in mine arms:
                    Leaps into the grave.

Now pile your dust, upon the quick, and dead,
Till of this flat a mountain you have made,
To o'ertop old Pelion, or the skyish head
Of blue Olympus.

HAMLET: What is he, whose griefs
Bear such an emphasis? whose phrase of sorrow
Conjures the wandering stars, and makes them stand
Like wonder-wounded hearers? This is I,
Hamlet the Dane.

Hamlet leaps in after Laertes.

LAERTES: The devil take thy soul.

HAMLET: Thou pray'st not well:
I prithee take thy fingers from my throat;
Sir, though I am not splenitive, and rash,
Yet have I something in me dangerous,
Which let thy wiseness fear. Away thy hand.

KING: Pluck them asunder.

QUEEN: Hamlet, Hamlet.

HORATIO: Good my Lord, be quiet.

HAMLET: Why I will fight with him upon this theme
Until my eyelids will no longer wag.

QUEEN: O my son, what theme?

HAMLET: I lov'd Ophelia; forty thousand brothers
Could not (with all their quantity of love)
Make up my sum. What wilt thou do for her?

KING: O he is mad Laertes.

QUEEN: For love of God forbear him.

HAMLET: Come show me what thou'lt do.
Woo't weep? woo't fight? woo't fast? woo't tear thy-
self?
Woo't drink up eisel, eat a crocodile?
I'll do't. Dost thou come here to whine;
To outface me with leaping in her grave?

Be buried quick with her, and so will I.
And if thou prate of mountains; let them throw
Millions of acres on us; till our ground
Singeing his pate against the burning zone,
Make Ossa like a wart. Nay, and thou'lt mouth,
I'll rant as well as thou.

QUEEN: This is mere madness:
And thus awhile the fit will work on him:
Anon as patient as the female dove,
When that her golden couplets are disclosed,
His silence will sit drooping.

HAMLET: Hear you sir:
What is the reason that you use me thus?
I lov'd you ever; but it is no matter:
Let Hercules himself do what he may,
The cat will mew, and dog will have his day.
Exit.

KING: I pray you good Horatio wait upon him:
Exit Horatio.
Strengthen your patience in our last night's speech,
We'll put the matter to the present push:
Good Gertrude set some watch over your son,
This grave shall have a living monument:
An hour of quiet shortly shall we see;
Till then, in patience our proceeding be.
Exeunt.

V.2

Enter Hamlet and Horatio.

HAMLET: So much for this sir; now shall you see the other,
You do remember all the circumstance?

HORATIO: Remember it my Lord?

HAMLET: Sir, in my heart there was a kind of fighting,
    That would not let me sleep; methought I lay
    Worse than the mutines in the bilboes, rashly,
    (And praised be rashness for it, let us know,
    Our indiscretion sometimes serves us well,
    When our deep plots do pall, and that should teach us,
    There's a Divinity that shapes our ends,
    Rough-hew them how we will) —
HORATIO: This is most certain.
HAMLET: Up from my cabin
    My sea-gown scarf'd about me in the dark,
    Grop'd I to find out them; had my desire,
    Finger'd their packet, and in fine, withdrew
    To mine own room again, making so bold,
    (My fears forgetting manners) to unseal
    Their grand commission, where I found Horatio,
    Oh royal knavery: an exact command,
    Larded with many several sorts of reasons;
    Importing Denmark's health, and England's too,
    With hoo, such bugs and goblins in my life,
    That on the supervise no leisure bated,
    No not to stay the grinding of the axe,
    My head should be struck off.
HORATIO: Is't possible?
HAMLET: Here's the commission, read it at more leisure:
    But wilt thou hear me how I did proceed?
HORATIO: I beseech you.
HAMLET: Being thus be-netted round with villains,
    Or I could make a prologue to my brains,
    They had begun the play. I sate me down,
    Devis'd a new commission, wrote it fair,
    I once did hold it as our statists do,
    A baseness to write fair: and labour'd much

How to forget that learning: but sir now,
It did me yeoman's service: wilt thou know
The effects of what I wrote?

HORATIO: Ay, good my Lord.

HAMLET: An earnest conjuration from the King,
As England was his faithful tributary,
As love between them, as the palm should flourish,
As Peace should still her wheaten garland wear,
And stand a comma 'tween their amities,
And many such-like As'es of great charge,
That on the view and know of these contents,
Without debatement further, more or less,
He should the bearers put to sudden death,
Not shriving-time allow'd.

HORATIO: How was this seal'd?

HAMLET: Why, even in that was Heaven ordinate;
I had my father's signet in my purse,
Which was the model of that Danish seal:
Folded the writ up in form of the other,
Subscrib'd it, gave't th' impression, plac'd it safely,
The changeling never known: now, the next day
Was our sea-fight, and what to this was sequent.
Thou know'st already.

HORATIO: So Guildenstern and Rosencrantz, go to't.

HAMLET: Why man, they did make love to this employ-
ment.
They are not near my conscience; their defeat
Doth by their own insinuation grow:
'Tis dangerous, when the baser nature comes
Between the pass, and fell incensed points
Of mighty opposites.

HORATIO. Why, what a King is this?

HAMLET: Does it not, thinks't thee, stand me now upon?

He that hath kill'd my King, and whor'd my mother,
Popp'd in between th' election and my hopes,
Thrown out his angle for my proper life,
And with such cozenage; is't not perfect conscience,
To quit him with this arm? and is't not to be damn'd
To let this canker of our nature come
In further evil?

HORATIO: It must be shortly known to him from England
What is the issue of the business there.

HAMLET: It will be short,
The interim's mine, and a man's life's no more
Than to say one: but I am very sorry good Horatio,
That to Laertes I forgot myself;
For by the image of my cause, I see
The portraiture of his; I'll court his favours:
But sure the bravery of his grief did put me
Into a towering passion.

HORATIO: Peace, who comes here?

Enter young Osric.

OSRIC: Your Lordship is right welcome back to Denmark.

HAMLET: I humbly thank you sir, dost know this water-fly?

HORATIO: No my good Lord.

HAMLET: Thy state is the more gracious; for 'tis a vice to know him: he hath much land, and fertile; let a beast be Lord of beasts, and his crib shall stand at the King's mess; 'tis a chough; but as I say, spacious in the possession of dirt.

OSRIC: Sweet Lord, if your friendship were at leisure, I should impart a thing to you from his Majesty.

HAMLET: I will receive it with all diligence of spirit; put your bonnet to his right use, 'tis for the head.

OSRIC: I thank your Lordship, it is very hot.

HAMLET: No, believe me 'tis very cold, the wind is northerly.

OSRIC: It is indifferent cold my Lord indeed.

HAMLET: Methinks it is very sultry, and hot for my complexion.

OSRIC: Exceedingly, my Lord, it is very sultry, as 'twere I cannot tell how: but my Lord, his Majesty bade me signify to you, that he has laid a great wager on your head: sir, this is the matter.

HAMLET: I beseech you remember.

OSRIC: Nay, in good faith, for mine ease in good faith: [sir here is newly come to Court Laertes, believe me an absolute gentleman, full of most excellent differences, of very soft society, and great showing: indeed to speak feelingly of him, he is the card or calendar of gentry: for you shall find in him the continent of what part a gentleman would see.

HAMLET: Sir, his definement suffers no perdition in you, though I know to divide him inventorially would dizzy th' arithmetic of memory, and yet but yaw neither in respect of his quick sail, but in the verity of extolment, I take him to be a soul of great article, and his infusion of such dearth and rareness, as to make true diction of him, his semblable is his mirror, and who else would trace him, his umbrage nothing more.

OSRIC: Your Lordship speaks most infallibly of him.

HAMLET: The concernancy sir, why do we wrap the gentleman in our more rawer breath?

OSRIC: Sir.

HORATIO: Is't not possible to understand in another tongue, you will to't sir really.

HAMLET: What imports the nomination of this gentleman?

OSRIC: Of Laertes?

HORATIO: His purse is empty already, all's golden words are spent.

HAMLET: Of him sir.

OSRIC: I know you are not ignorant.

HAMLET: I would you did sir, yet in faith if you did, it would not much approve me, well sir?]

OSRIC: You are not ignorant of what excellence Laertes is.

[**HAMLET**: I dare not confess that, lest I should compare with him in excellence, but to know a man well, were to know himself.

OSRIC: I mean sir for his weapon, but in the imputation laid on him, by them in his meed, he's unfellowed.]

HAMLET: What's his weapon?

OSRIC: Rapier and dagger.

HAMLET: That's two of his weapons; but well.

OSRIC: The King sir has wager'd with him six Barbary horses, against the which he impon'd as I take it, six French rapiers and poniards, with their assigns, as girdle, hangers or so: three of the carriages in faith are very dear to fancy, very responsive to the hilts, most delicate carriages, and of very liberal conceit.

HAMLET: What call you the carriages?

[**HORATIO**: I knew you must be edified by the margent ere you had done.]

OSRIC: The carriages sir, are the hangers.

HAMLET: The phrase would be more germane to the matter, if we could carry cannon by our sides; I would it might be hangers till then; but on, six Barbary horses against six French swords, their assigns, and three liberal-conceited carriages, that's the French bet against the Danish, why is this impon'd as you call it?

OSRIC: The King sir, hath laid that in a dozen passes between yourself and him, he shall not exceed you three hits; he hath laid on twelve for nine, and that would come to immediate trial, if your Lordship would vouchsafe the answer.

HAMLET: How if I answer no?

OSRIC: I mean my Lord, the opposition of your person in trial.

HAMLET: Sir, I will walk here in the Hall; if it please his Majesty, it is the breathing time of day with me; let the foils be brought, the gentleman willing, and the King hold his purpose; I will win for him if I can: if not, I will gain nothing but my shame, and the odd hits.

OSRIC: Shall I redeliver you e'en so?

HAMLET: To this effect sir, after what flourish your nature will.

OSRIC: I commend my duty to your Lordship.

Exit.

HAMLET: Yours, yours; he does well to commend it himself, there are no tongues else for's turn.

HORATIO: This lapwing runs away with the shell on his head.

HAMLET: He did comply with his dug before he suck'd it: thus has he and many more of the same bevy that I know the drossy age dotes on, only got the tune of the time, and outward habit of encounter, a kind of yesty collection, which carries them through and through the most fond and winnowed opinions; and do but blow them to their trials: the bubbles are out.

[*Enter a Lord.*

LORD: My Lord, his Majesty commended him to you by young Osric, who brings back to him that you attend him in the Hall. He sends to know if your pleasure hold to play with Laertes, or that you will take longer time?

HAMLET: I am constant to my purposes, they follow the

King's pleasure, if his fitness speaks, mine is ready; now or whensoever, provided I be so able as now.

LORD: The King, and Queen, and all are coming down.

HAMLET: In happy time.

LORD: The Queen desires you to use some gentle entertainment to Laertes, before you fall to play.

HAMLET: She well instructs me.

Exit Lord.]

HORATIO: You will lose this wager, my Lord.

HAMLET: I do not think so, since he went into France, I have been in continual practice; I shall win at the odds: but thou wouldst not think how ill all's here about my heart: but it is no matter.

HORATIO: Nay, good my Lord.

HAMLET: It is but foolery; but it is such a kind of gain-giving, as would perhaps trouble a woman.

HORATIO: If your mind dislike any thing, obey. I will forestal their repair hither, and say you are not fit.

HAMLET: Not a whit, we defy augury; there is special providence in the fall of a sparrow. If it be now, 'tis not to come: if it be not to come, it will be now: if it be not now, yet it will come; the readiness is all, since no man has aught of what he leaves. What is't to leave betimes?

Enter trumpets, drums and officer with cushion; King, Queen, and all the State; Attendants with foils and daggers; Laertes; a table prepared and flagons of wine on it.

KING: Come Hamlet, come, and take this hand from me.

HAMLET: Give me your pardon sir, I've done you wrong,
But pardon't as you are a gentleman.
This presence knows,
And you must needs have heard how I am punish'd
With sore distraction: What I have done
That might your nature, honour and exception

Roughly awake, I here proclaim was madness:
Was't Hamlet wrong'd Laertes? Never Hamlet.
If Hamlet from himself be ta'en away:
And when he's not himself, does wrong Laertes,
Then Hamlet does it not, Hamlet denies it:
Who does it then? His madness. If't be so,
Hamlet is of the faction that is wrong'd,
His madness is poor Hamlet's enemy.
Sir, in this audience,
Let my disclaiming from a purpos'd evil,
Free me so far in your most generous thoughts,
That I have shot mine arrow o'er the house,
And hurt my brother.

LAERTES: I am satisfied in Nature,
Whose motive in this case should stir me most
To my revenge. But in my terms of Honour
I stand aloof, and will no reconcilement,
Till by some elder masters of known honour,
I have a voice, and precedent of peace
To keep my name ungor'd. But till that time,
I do receive your offer'd love like love,
And will not wrong it.

HAMLET: I do embrace it freely,
And will this brother's wager frankly play.
Give us the foils: come on.

LAERTES: Come, one for me.

HAMLET: I'll be your foil Laertes, in mine ignorance
Your skill shall like a star i' th' darkest night,
Stick fiery off indeed.

LAERTES: You mock me sir.

HAMLET: No by this hand.

KING: Give them the foils young Osric, Cousin Hamlet.
You know the wager.

HAMLET: Very well my Lord,
  Your Grace hath laid the odds a' th' weaker side.
KING: I do not fear it, I have seen you both:
  But since he is better'd, we have therefore odds.
LAERTES: This is too heavy, let me see another.
HAMLET: This likes me well, these foils have all a length.
                 They prepare to play.
OSRIC: Ay my good Lord.
KING: Set me the stoups of wine upon that table:
  If Hamlet give the first, or second hit,
  Or quit in answer of the third exchange,
  Let all the battlements their ordnance fire,
  The King shall drink to Hamlet's better breath,
  And in the cup an union shall he throw
  Richer than that, which four successive Kings
  In Denmark's Crown have worn. Give me the cups.
  And let the kettle to the trumpets speak,
  The trumpet to the cannoneer without,
  The cannons to the heavens, the heaven to earth,
  Now the King drinks to Hamlet. Come, begin,
  And you the judges bear a wary eye.
                 Trumpets the while.
HAMLET: Come on sir.
LAERTES: Come my Lord.
                 They play.
HAMLET: One.
LAERTES: No.
HAMLET: Judgement.
OSRIC: A hit, a very palpable hit.
LAERTES: Well: again.
KING: Stay, give me drink. Hamlet, this pearl is thine,
  Here's to thy health. Give him the cup.
  Drums, trumpets and shot. Flourish. A piece goes off.

HAMLET: I'll play this bout first, set by awhile.
  Come: another hit; what say you?
LAERTES: A touch, a touch, I do confess.
KING: Our son shall win.
QUEEN: He's fat, and scant of breath.
  Here Hamlet take my napkin, rub thy brows:
  The Queen carouses to thy fortune, Hamlet.
HAMLET: Good Madam.
KING: Gertrude, do not drink.
QUEEN: I will my Lord; I pray you pardon me.
KING: It is the poison'd cup, it is too late.
HAMLET: I dare not drink yet Madam, by and by.
QUEEN: Come, let me wipe thy face.
LAERTES: My Lord, I'll hit him now.
KING: I do not think't.
LAERTES: And yet it is almost against my conscience.
HAMLET: Come for the third. Laertes, you but dally,
  I pray you pass with your best violence,
  I am afear'd you make a wanton of me.
LAERTES: Say you so? come on.
                    They play.
OSRIC: Nothing neither way.
LAERTES: Have at you now.
*In scuffling they catch one another's rapiers and both are
                    wounded.*
KING: Part them, they are incens'd.
HAMLET: Nay come, again.
        Laertes falls down; the Queen falls down, dying.
OSRIC: Look to the Queen there hoa.
HORATIO: They bleed on both sides. How is't my Lord?
OSRIC: How is't Laertes.
LAERTES: Why as a woodcock to mine own springe, Osric,
  I am justly kill'd with mine own treachery.

HAMLET: How does the Queen?

KING: She sounds to see them bleed.

QUEEN: No, no, the drink, the drink. O my dear Hamlet,
The drink, the drink, I am poison'd.
                              Dies.

HAMLET: O villainy! How? let the door be lock'd.
Treachery, seek it out.

LAERTES: It is here Hamlet. Hamlet, thou art slain,
No medicine in the world can do thee good.
In thee, there is not half an hour of life;
The treacherous instrument is in thy hand,
Unbated and envenom'd: the foul practice
Hath turn'd itself on me. Lo, here I lie,
Never to rise again: thy mother's poison'd:
I can no more, the King, the King's to blame.

HAMLET: The point envenom'd too,
Then venom to thy work.
                    Stabs the King.

ALL: Treason, treason.

KING: O yet defend me friends, I am but hurt.

HAMLET: Here thou incestuous, murderous, damned Dane,
Drink off this potion: is thy union here?
Follow my mother.
                    King dies.

LAERTES: He is justly serv'd.
It is a poison temper'd by himself:
Exchange forgiveness with me, noble Hamlet;
Mine and my father's death come not upon thee,
Nor thine on me.
                    Dies.

HAMLET: Heaven make thee free of it, I follow thee.
I am dead Horatio, wretched Queen adieu.
You look that pale, and tremble at this chance,

That are but mutes or audience to this act:
Had I but time (as this fell Sergeant Death
Is strict in his arrest) O I could tell you.
But let it be: Horatio, I am dead,
Thou liv'st, report me and my cause aright
To the unsatisfied.

HORATIO: Never believe it.
I am more an antique Roman than a Dane:
Here's yet some liquor left.

HAMLET: As th'art a man,
Give me the cup. Let go, by Heaven I'll have't.
O good Horatio, what a wounded name,
(Things standing thus unknown) shall live behind me.
If thou didst ever hold me in thy heart,
Absent thee from felicity awhile,
And in this harsh world draw thy breath in pain,
To tell my story.
                    March afar off, and shot within.
What warlike noise is this?
                    Enter Osric.

OSRIC: Young Fortinbras, with conquest come from Poland
To th' Ambassadors of England gives
This warlike volley.

HAMLET: O I die Horatio:
The potent poison quite o'er-crows my spirit,
I cannot live to hear the news from England,
But I do prophesy th' election lights
On Fortinbras, he has my dying voice
So tell him with the occurrents more and less,
Which have solicited. The rest is silence.
                    Dies.

HORATIO: Now cracks a noble heart: good night sweet
    Prince,

And flights of Angels sing thee to thy rest.
Why does the drum come hither?
Enter Fortinbras and English Ambassadors, with drums,
colours, and Attendants.
FORTINBRAS: Where is this sight?
HORATIO: What is it you would see;
If aught of woe, or wonder, cease your search.
FORTINBRAS: This quarry cries on havoc. O proud death,
What feast is toward in thine eternal cell,
That thou so many Princes, at a shot,
So bloodily hast struck?
FIRST AMBASSADOR: The sight is dismal,
And our affairs from England come too late,
The ears are senseless that should give us hearing,
To tell him his commandment is fulfill'd,
That Rosencrantz and Guildenstern are dead:
Where should we have our thanks?
HORATIO: Not from his mouth,
Had it th' ability of life to thank you:
He never gave commandment for their death.
But since so jump upon this bloody question,
You from the Polack wars, and you from England
Are here arriv'd, give order that these bodies
High on a stage be placed to the view,
And let me speak to th' yet unknowing world,
How these things came about. So shall you hear
Of carnal, bloody, and unnatural acts,
Of accidental judgements, casual slaughters,
Of deaths put on by cunning, and forc'd cause,
And in this upshot, purposes mistook,
Fall'n on the inventors' heads. All this can I
Truly deliver.
FORTINBRAS: Let us haste to hear it,

And call the noblest to the audience.
For me, with sorrow, I embrace my fortune,
I have some rights of memory in this Kingdom,
Which now to claim my vantage doth invite me.

HORATIO: Of that I shall have also cause to speak,
And from his mouth whose voice will draw no more:
But let this same be presently perform'd,
Even while men's minds are wild, lest some mischance
On plots, and errors happen.

FORTINBRAS: Let four captains
Bear Hamlet like a soldier to the stage,
For he was likely, had he been put on
To have prov'd most royally: and for his passage,
The soldiers' music, and the rites of war
Speak loudly for him.
Take up the body; such a sight as this
Becomes the field, but here shows much amiss.
Go, bid the soldiers shoot.

> *Exeunt marching: after the which a peal of ordnance
> are shot off.*

NOTES

References are to the page and line of this edition;
there are 33 lines to the full page.

Long live the King: the watchword for the night.   P. 25 L. 4

approve our eyes: corroborate what we have seen.   P. 26 L. 10

Thou art a scholar: As a scholar Horatio would know   P. 26 L. 27
Latin and the proper form of ecclesiastical exorcism.

fair ... buried Denmark: i.e. the outward resemblance   P. 26 L. 33
to the King lately dead.

sensible and true avouch: testimony truly perceived.   P. 27 L. 13

sledded poleaxe: This is one of the famous cruxes in   P. 27 L. 20
Hamlet. The Folio reads 'sledded Pollax'; both
Quartos 'sleaded pollax'; modern editors 'sledded
Polacks'. It thus remains doubtful whether the late
King smote the 'Poles in their sledges' or smote the
ice with his 'heavy (leaded) poleaxe'. Poleaxe is
probably correct, for the axe was the national
weapon of the Danes; as Nashe sneered: 'The most
gross and sense-less proud dolts ... are the Danes, who
stand so much upon their unwieldy burly-boned
soldiery, that they account of no man that hath not
a battle axe at his girdle to hough dogs with.' (*Piers
Penniless,* 1591, ed. R. B. McKerrow, i, 177.)

gross and scope: general conclusion.   P. 27 L. 28

So nightly ... day: i.e. workers in shipyards and   P. 27 L. 32
munition factories are working night shifts and Sundays; a sure sign that this hasty accumulation of
munitions is for a war. Thus on 21st June, 1594,
Ralegh reported that a surprise was expected from
the Spanish Fleet at Brest 'for the carpenters and all
others about the fleet work on the Sabbath day'.
(*I Elizabethan Journal,* p. 305.)

P. 28 L. 14   *Seal'd compact:* formal agreement.

P. 28 L. 15   *heraldry:* because the heralds were responsible for arranging formal combats of honour.

P. 28 L. 18   *moiety competent:* adequate portion.

P. 28 L. 22   *carriage of the article design'd:* intention proposed by the clause in the agreement.

P. 28 L. 26   *landless resolutes:* adventurers (such as Essex's followers had been), with no landed property, and therefore ready for any desperate enterprise.

P. 29 L. 7   *A moth it is:* Here Horatio the scholar speaks from his reading of Roman history.

P. 29 L. 12   *As stars with trains of fire:* The sense of this passage is broken: probably a line has been left out.

P. 29 L. 13   *moist star:* the moon, which governs the tides.

P. 29 L. 17   *harbingers:* literally officials sent ahead to make preparations when the Court went on progress.

P. 29 L. 23   *Stay illusion ... speak.* According to contemporary belief, the appearance of a spirit or wraith 'in the shadow of a person newly dead' was evil. 'Amongst the Gentiles the Devil used that much to make them believe that it was some good spirit that appeared to them then, either to forewarn them of the death of their friend, or else to discover unto them the will of the defunct, or what was the way of his slaughter. ... And this way he easily deceived the Gentiles because they knew not God: and to that same effect is it, that he now appears in that manner to some ignorant Christians. For he dare not so illude that any that knoweth that, neither can the spirit of the defunct return to his friend, or yet an angel use such forms.' (*Daemonology*, 1597, Book III, Chap. i.) To reveal buried treasure was a further reason. Horatio thus adjures the Ghost by three potent reasons, but before he can mention the fourth (and true) cause of its uneasiness, the cock crows.

partisan: long handled spear, with curved blades pro- P. 30 L. 5
jecting at the base of the spearhead.

planets strike: planets were supposed to bring dis- P. 30 L. 30
aster.

dilated articles: detailed instructions. It was customary P. 32 L. 23
to provide ambassadors with (a) detailed instructions
for their guidance, (b) formal letters of introduction
and greeting for the foreign King, (c) a personal letter
to the King.

A little more than kin, and less than kind: too near a P. 33 L. 21
relation (uncle-father) but far from dear.

obsequious sorrow: literally, 'suitable for obsequies'. P. 34 L. 16

You are the most immediate to our Throne: As is obvious P. 34 L. 33
from the play, Shakespeare regarded the throne of
Denmark as elective. Critics have unnecessarily as-
sumed that Elizabethan playgoers would have been
puzzled by such a procedure. They were quite
familiar with the story. Nor were elective monar-
chies unknown. When the luckless ambassador from
Poland ventured on his master's behalf to criticize
Queen Elizabeth face to face in 1597, she retorted
that his King was evidently an ignorant young man,
'*non de iure sanguinis, sed iure electionis, immo noviter
electus*' (being chosen not by right of blood but by
right of election, and newly at that).

great cannon to the clouds: These cannonadings were a P. 35 L. 17
Danish custom. When in 1606 the Danish King
came to visit James I, he received King James on
board his ship, and 'at every health there were from
the ships of Denmark and the forts some three or
four score great shot discharged; and of these thundering vollies there were between 40 and 50'.
(Nichols' *Progresses of James I*, ii, 92.)

too too solid flesh: Both Quartos read 'sallied'= P. 35 L. 21
'sullied', or 'smirched', which may be correct;

though there was nothing comic to Shakespeare's audience in the phrase 'solid flesh'.

P. 36 L. 8   *Niobe:* she boasted of her children to the annoyance of the Goddess Artemis, who slew them. Niobe was so sorrowful that she was changed into a fountain.

P. 36 L. 9   *discourse of reason:* power of speech.

P. 37 L. 9   *Thrift, thrift ... marriage tables:* 'for economy's sake the remains of the funeral feast were sent up cold for the marriage breakfast'.

P. 38 L. 13   *platform:* place where the cannon were mounted.

P. 39 L. 2   *beaver:* front part of the helmet which at this period could be raised, enabling the warrior's face to be seen within.

P. 40 L. 15   *toy in blood:* trifling impulse.

P. 40 L. 18   *suppliance of a minute:* momentary.

P. 40 L. 28   *his greatness weighed:* when you consider his position

P. 41 L. 31   *wreaks not his own rede:* does not follow his own counsel.

P. 42 L. 11   *their adoption tried:* tried by adopting.

P. 42 L. 13   *dull thy palm, with entertainment:* make callous by greeting everyone.

P. 42 L. 14   *comrade:* the Quarto reads 'courage' (=hothead), which may be right.

P. 42 L. 23   *Or of a most select and generous, chief in that:* This is the Quarto reading and has the advantage of making sense. The Folio reads 'Are of a most select and generous cheff in that.' Englishman had a good opportunity of observing French fashions in August, 1601, when the Marshal Biron came over with a large following to visit Queen Elizabeth. It was 'much noted that they all wore black with no kind of bravery at all, wherefore Sir Walter Ralegh rode by night to London to provide himself with a plain black taffeta suit and a black saddle' (*Last Elizabethan Journal*, p. 201). Biron was executed a year

later and the event was dramatized by the Admiral's
Men, who purchased black for the costumes.

command to parley: i.e. when he entreats you to see P. 44 L. 10
him do not regard it as a command to surrender.

bawds: Folio and Quartos read 'bonds', an easy mis- P. 44 L. 17
print for 'bauds' the Elizabethan spelling for
'bawds'.

But to my mind …: This speech is cut in the Folio; P. 45 L. 14
either it was too long, or with the coming of James's
Queen Anne (who was a Dane) to England it was
considered tactless.

pith … attribute: i.e. we lose the essential part of our P. 45 L. 22
honour because of our reputations as drunkards.

complexion: The four 'humours' of which the body P. 45 L. 27
was supposed to consist maintained health so long as
they were evenly balanced; but if one predominated,
then temperament and complexion revealed the excess in a mood and countenance which was sanguine,
melancholic, choleric or phlegmatic.

nature's livery: i.e. inborn. P. 45 L. 32

fortune's star: acquired by ill luck. P. 45 L. 32

the dram of eale … own scandal: This is the most dis- P. 46 L. 3
puted passage in all Shakespeare. Though the text is
corrupt, the meaning is clear: 'a small proportion of
evil will bring scandal on the whole substance however noble'. *eale:* evil.

spirit of health or Goblin damn'd: from the first Ham- P. 46 L. 9
let is uncertain whether the Ghost is a benign or an
evil spirit. See note on p. 29, l. 23, and p. 78, l. 22.

canoniz'd: buried according to the canon of the P. 46 L. 16
church.

cerements: the waxen coverings in which the bodies P. 46 L. 17
of the illustrious dead were wrapped.

pin's fee: worth a pin. P. 46 L. 5

sovereignty of reason: rule of reason. P. 47 L. 14

P. 47 L. 16   *toys of desperation*: desperate fancies.

P. 47 L. 27   *Nemean lion*: the destruction of this beast was one of the twelve labours of Hercules.

P. 49 L. 3   *eternal blazon*: description of eternity.

P. 49 L. 17   *Lethe*: the river of forgetfulness in the underworld.

P. 49 L. 21   *forged process*: false account.

P. 50 L. 3   *Upon a wretch whose natural gifts were poor ... mine*: Both Hamlet and the Ghost insist that Claudius is physically insignificant; Gertrude's adultery is thus the more monstrous. On the stage however the King is usually presented as a fine and handsome man.

P. 50 L. 6   *shape of Heaven*: disguised as an angel.

P. 50 L. 13   *secure hour*: period of relaxation.

P. 50 L. 21   *eager droppings*: sour, or acid, substance added to.

P. 50 L. 23   *tetter bak'd about*: crusted over with blotches.

P. 50 L. 29   *Unhousel'd, disappointed, unaneled*: unfortified by the last Sacrament, unprepared, without supreme unction. See later note on p. 101, l. 23.

P. 51 L. 18   *distracted globe*: i.e. his head.

P. 51 L. 19   *table*: note book. Intellectual young gentlemen carried 'tables' with them to take down good sayings, sermons, speeches and anecdotes. See note on p. 86, l. 22.

P. 51 L. 31   *to my word*: for my cue.

P. 52 L. 8   *Hillo, ho, ho*: the falconer's cry.

P. 53 L. 18   *Upon my sword*: by the cross made by the hilt of the sword; but for soldiers the sword itself is a sacred emblem.

P. 55   *II. i.* The purpose of this scene is to show that some time has elapsed. Laertes has now been in Paris for several weeks.

P. 55 L. 20   *come you ... touch it*: 'you get nearer by indirect than by direct questioning.'

P. 56 L. 4   *fencing*: a young man who haunted fencing schools was likely to be quarrelsome and one of the sporting set.

open to incontinency: it is open scandal that disturbs the P. 56 L. 10 politician.

fetch of warrant: a trick which has been found to work. P. 56 L. 21

at tennis: a natural form of exercise for Laertes in P. 57 L. 10 Paris. 'As for the exercise of Tennis play ... Methinks it is also strange how apt they be here to play well, that ye would think they were born with rackets in their hands, even the children themselves manage them so well, and some of their women also, as we observed at Blois.' (Robert Dallington, *The View of France*, 1604). In England tennis was a courtiers' game.

assays of bias: indirect approaches, as in a game of P. 57 L. 16 bowls where the bowl takes a curved course.

Lord Hamlet ... before me: Hamlet thus shows all P. 58 L. 1 the signs of a lover who has fallen into extremes of love melancholy, the outward signs of which, as Rosalind told Orlando, are:– a lean cheek, a blue eye and sunken, an unquestionable spirit, a beard neglected, 'then your hose should be ungartered, your bonnet unbanded, your sleeve unbuttoned, your shoe untied, and everything about you demonstrating a careless desolation'. (*As You Like It*, III. ii. 400.)

doublet all unbrac'd: the doublet (short close-fitting P. 58 L. 1 jacket) was attached to the hose (breeches) with laces. When a man was careless of his appearance, he 'unbraced' i.e. loosed the laces.

down-gyved: hanging round his ankles like fetters. P. 58 L. 3

full bent: stretched tight – like a bow. P. 60 L. 20

fruit to that great feast: the dessert coming at the end. P. 61 L. 14

borne in hand: imposed upon. P. 61 L. 32

assay of arms: attempt by force of arms. P. 62 L. 3

P. 62 L. 21   *expostulate*: indulge in academic discussion.

P. 63 L. 28   *whilst this machine is to him*: Hamlet writes in the
ornate style affected by Elizabethan gallants.

P. 64 L. 10   *play'd the desk or table-book*: acted as winking agent –
desks and books being natural post-offices for love-
letters.

P. 65 L. 3   *Centre*: the centre of the Earth which was regarded
as the absolute centre of the Universe.

P. 66 L. 1   *Sun breed maggots*: this was very generally believed.

P. 66 L. 2   *good kissing carrion*: good kissable flesh. Quarto and
Folio both read 'good'. Some editors emend to
'God'.

P. 67 L. 13   *good lads*: how do ye both? The conversation between the three young men which follows is typical
court wit – quick, witty and full of double meaning.

P. 67 L. 15   *indifferent*: neither too happy, nor too sad.

P. 67 L. 28   *Let me question*: From this point to p. 68, l. 25, the
Folio gives a fuller version of this dialogue.

P. 68 L. 8   *Why ... ambition*: Rosencrantz is feeling after the
likeliest cause of Hamlet's melancholy – thwarted
ambition.

P. 68 L. 25   *most dreadfully attended*: my servants are few and in-
competent, or 'I am oppressed by fancies'.

P. 69 L. 18   *moult no feather*: i.e. you will not be obliged to betray
the King's secrets.

P. 69 L. 21   *this goodly frame the earth*: It is probable that this passage was suggested to Shakespeare by William
Parry's *A new and large discourse of the travels of Sir
Anthony Shirley* which came out in the autumn of
1601, and was much read. Parry praising travel
wrote: 'To see those resplendent and crystalline
heavens over-canopying the earth, invested most
sumptuously in height of Nature's pride with her
richest livery, the particularities whereof, were they
described according to the truth of their nature, it

might breed a scruple in natural Man whether Man
were, for transgression, ever unimparadised or no.'

quintessence: the fifth essence, the ultimate quest of P. 69 L. 31
alchemists; it was the substance which would remain
when the four elements of matter had been ab-
stracted.

humorous man: not the funny man of the party but P. 70 L. 12
the man who took the 'character' parts. The melancholy Jacques is a perfect example of a 'humorous'
man whilst Falstaff and his gang are labelled 'irregu-
lar humorists' in the Folio.

sere: The sere is part of the trigger mechanism of a P. 70 L. 14
rifle. 'Tickle o' the sere'=which explode at a touch.

innovation: riot, revolution. This passage seems a P. 70. L. 21
clear reference to the rebellion of the Earl of Essex
in which Shakespeare's company were somewhat
implicated because they played *Richard II* at the request of Essex's friends the day before the rebellion.
There is no record that the theatres were closed after
the rebellion, but it was usual to 'inhibit' playing at
times of crisis – as happened in March, 1603, when
Queen Elizabeth was dying.

Nay, their endeavour ... Hercules and his load too. This P. 70 L. 26
passage, which is added in the Folio, refers to the
war of the Theatres of 1599–1601. For two years Ben
Jonson (writing for the Children of Blackfriars) and
Marston (writing for the Children of Paul's) attacked
each other in successive plays. The war was ended in
the autumn of 1601 when Jonson, having thought to
end the matter by *Poetaster*, was finally suppressed by
Dekker's *Satiromastix*.

cry out on the top of question: perhaps 'speak in a P. 70 L. 28
shrill key', or 'cry out the latest detail of the dispute'.

many wearing rapiers, are afraid of goosequills: i.e. many P. 70 L. 30
gallants are afraid of being satirized by the dramatists.

There was much cynical and satirical caricature in the plays of the Stage War. The adult professional players were greatly affected by the excitement which took away their best audiences.

P. 71 L. 6   *succession*: i.e. the profession which they will one day follow.

P. 71 L. 16   *Hercules and his load*: the Globe Theatre bore as its sign Hercules carrying the world with the motto *Totus mundus agit histrionem*.

P. 71 L. 27   *appurtenance ... ceremony*: formal ceremony (e.g. shaking hands) is the natural accompaniment of welcome.

P. 72 L. 1   *North-north-west*: i.e. $337\frac{1}{2}°$ of the compass.

P. 72 L. 2   *handsaw*: either a corruption for 'heronshaw'= a heron; or 'hawk' means a tool, like a pickaxe. Either way the general meaning is 'I'm not so mad as you think.'

P. 72 L. 14   *Roscius*: a famous Roman actor.

P. 72 L. 20   *The best actors in the world*: Polonius is reading out a playbill which the players have given him detailing their excellencies. The licence issued to the Chamberlain's Company when they became the King's players on 19th May, 1603, permitted them 'freely to use and exercise the art and faculty of playing comedies, tragedies, histories, interludes, morals, pastorals, stage plays and such others.'

P. 72 L. 23   *Scene individable*: where the action takes place in one spot as opposed to 'Poem unlimited' which allowed many scenes.

P. 72 L. 24   *Seneca ... Plautus*: the two Latin dramatists with which every educated man had been painfully familiarized in his school days.

P. 73 L. 16   *chopine*: a kind of lady's shoe with a very thick sole of cork. The boy of the travelling company who takes the women's parts has grown considerably, for

chopines are from 4 to 15 inches high. (For an illus-
tration see M. C. Linthicum. *Costume in Elizabethan
Drama*, p. 250.)

crack'd within the ring: Before coins were milled on P. 73 L. 18
the rim, they were liable to crack. When the crack
reached the ring surrounding the device, they were
no longer good.

caviary to the general: i.e. a delicacy too refined for P. 73 L. 25
the vulgar.

Hyrcanian beast: tiger. P. 74 L. 5

The rugged Pyrrhus ... in the gods: This speech is in P. 74 L. 5
the heavy style which was still popular in the dramas
of the rival company, the Admiral's Men, under the
great tragic actor, Edward Alleyn. Both in the hyper-
bolical diction and the passionate action the First
Player imitates the Alleyn manner.

ominous horse: i.e. the Wooden Horse by which the P. 74 L. 9
Greeks at last entered Troy.

heraldry: i.e. painting. P. 74 L. 11

proof eterne: everlasting protection. P. 75 L. 11

abstracts and brief chronicles of the time: Elizabethan P. 76 L. 15
players enacted history and contemporary events as
closely as they dared, and were often in trouble for
their comments on their betters. In 1600, in the time
of his disgrace, Essex moaned 'The prating tavern
haunter speaks of me what he lists: they print me
and make me speak to the world, and shortly they
will play me upon the stage.'

God buy ye: God be with you. P. 77 L. 6

dream of passion: imaginary emotion. P. 77 L. 9

muddy-mettled: made of mud – not iron. P. 77 L. 24

unpregnant of my cause: barren of plans for my re- P. 77 L. 25
venge.

that guilty creatures ... proclaim'd their malefactions: P. 78 L. 13
Modern psychologists, accepting this fact, have

devised delicate apparatus for recording the re-
actions.

P. 78 L. 22   *The Spirit . . . the Devil:* See note on p. 29, l. 23.

P. 78 L. 25   *Out of my weakness, and my melancholy:* Hamlet knows
that he is suffering from melancholy, which in its
extreme forms caused terrible visions and hallucina-
tions. 'Even as slime and dirt in a standing puddle
engender toads and frogs and many other unsightly
creatures, so this slimy melancholy humour still
thickening as it stands still engendreth many mis-
shapen objects in our imaginations.' (Thomas Nash.
Terrors of the Night, 1593. ed. R. B. McKerrow, i,
345.) It was natural therefore for Hamlet to suspect
either that he had been deceived by the Devil or by
hallucination, and to seek some reliable corrobora-
tion of his ghostly visitation.

P. 78 L. 27   *Abuses me to damn me:* tempts me to commit mortal
sin.

P. 78 L. 28   *relative:* i.e. convincing than an apparition.

P. 79 L. 17   *forcing of his disposition:* forcing himself to be civil.

P. 79 L. 18   *Niggard of question:* not asking many questions.

P. 80 L. 1   *give him a further edge:* whet him on.

P. 80 L. 25   *read on this book:* i.e. a Book of Devotions.

P. 80 L. 28   *Devotions visage:* an outward appearance of religion.

P. 81 L. 7   *To be, or not to be:* Hamlet is reading his book,
brooding over its contents, as the King's remark in
the First Quarto shows – 'See where he comes poring
upon a book.' He is thus too much absorbed to
notice Ophelia. The whole speech epitomizes the
sense of disillusion and futility which was common
amongst thinking men at this time. Its agnosticism
is worth noting: Hamlet is not afraid of death, provided it be an eternal sleep, but of the future of end-
less nightmare. This speech gives a picture of Hamlet
the scholar.

mortal coil: fuss of life.   P. 81 L. 18

native hue ... cast of thought: natural courage is sickened P. 82 L. 2
by the thought of the hereafter.

nunnery: i.e. a place where she will be free from P. 83 L. 8
temptation.

Where's your father?: This whole episode between P. 83 L. 17
Hamlet and Ophelia puzzles and disturbs critics. The
explanation is perhaps simple. When Ophelia, at the
bidding of Polonius, rejects Hamlet, his first and
natural thought is that some other suitor has dis-
placed him, which is apparently confirmed when
Ophelia hands back his gifts. As he grows vehement
in this speech, he notices a movement in the arras,
and realizes that there is an eavesdropper. 'Where's
your father?' he asks. 'At home, my Lord,' Ophelia
lies. Then, thinks Hamlet, it must be the lover.
Hence his increasing bitterness; for Ophelia as well
as his mother, has now revealed the rottenness of her
sex.

nickname God's creatures ... ignorance: you call things P. 83 L. 32
by indecent names, and pretend to be too simple to
realize their meanings.

hatch, and the disclose: when the chicks are revealed. P. 84 L. 23

Speak the speech ...: This passage is Shakespeare's P. 85 L. 17
contribution to the contemporary controversies on
stagecraft, and states the creed and practice of his
own company contrasted with the ranting methods
of Alleyn and his fellows. Alleyn was notable for such
parts as Tamburlane, Orlando Furioso, Dr Faustus,
the Jew of Malta, and Hieronimo, the distracted
father in the *Spanish Tragedy*. As Tamburlane he
'bent his brows and fetched his stations up and down'
with furious gestures.

groundlings: the poorer spectators who stood in the P. 85 L. 26
yard.

P. 85 L. 27 *inexplicable dumb-shows:* The dumb-show was an old-fashioned device still used by the Admiral's Men, but not by Shakespeare. Before a tragedy, and sometimes before each act, the characters silently mimed the action to follow.

P. 85 L. 29 *Termagant:* the god of the Saracens, shown on the stage as a violent and ranting person, as also was Herod.

P. 86 L. 5 *the purpose of playing:* Shakespeare's words completely contradict those who suppose that he was too lofty or too timid to have any thought for events of his own time in his plays.

P. 86 L. 18 *Nature's journeymen:* hired workmen, not master craftsmen.

P. 86 L. 22 *let those that play your Clowns:* Both the attack on the ranting tragedian and the conceited clown are directed against individuals. The latter is obviously Will Kempe, the most popular of Elizabethan clowns. He had joined the Chamberlain's Men in 1594, but left them in 1599 about the time that they occupied the new Globe Theatre. He then went abroad, but came back in the autumn of 1601, and joined Worcester's players, then acting at the Rose Theatre, almost next door to the Globe: hence Shakespeare's particular annoyance. In the pirated First Quarto there is an additional passage:

'And then you have some again that keep one suit of jests, as a man is known by one suit of apparel, and gentlemen quote his jests down in their tables before they come to the play, as thus: "Cannot you stay till I eat my porridge?" and "You owe me a quarter's wages," and "My coat wants a cullison," and "Your beer is sour," and blabbering with his lips, and thus keeping in his cinquepace of jests, when God knows the warm clown cannot make a jest unless by chance, as the blind man catcheth a hare. Masters tell him of it.'

As Kempe had died between the issue of the pirated Quarto and the Second Quarto the passage was expunged.

candied tongue: the tongue sugared over with hypocrisy. P. 87 L. 18

unkennel: bring to light; used of forcing a fox out of its hole. P. 88 L. 6

damned ghost: Hamlet is still not sure whether the ghost was a good or an evil spirit. P. 88 L. 7

chameleon's dish: the chameleon was supposed to eat air. P. 88 L. 23

jig-maker: a jig was a little after-piece, usually bawdy, which followed the play, a mixture of song, dance and pantomime. P. 89 L. 21

I'll have a suit of sables: Hamlet is punning on the double meaning of sable fur and sable (= black). The suit of sables is the gown trimmed with fur of prosperous old gentlemen, still worn on civic occasions by members of the City companies. Hamlet means 'it is so long ago that I must have become elderly and respectable.' P. 89 L. 27

the hobby-horse: a figure in the country dances and May games which were now out of favour with the godly. P. 89 L. 31

For O, for O: the refrain from a popular ballad. P. 89 L. 32

The dumb-show: Critics have been disturbed because this dumb-show preceding a play cannot exactly be paralleled with any other Elizabethan play, and also because the King fails to appreciate the significance of it. Shakespeare's intention however was to present a stagey play in order to bring about sufficient contrast. Dumb shows, as Hamlet said, were often inexplicable. This dumb show puzzles Ophelia. P. 89 L. 33

P. 90 L. 30   *posy of a ring*: rings given as personal gifts often were inscribed with pretty messages, which of necessity were short.

P. 91 L. 3   *Full thirty times … sacred bands*: A parody of bombastic dramatic diction. The player-king is merely saying, 'My dear, we have been married thirty years.'

P. 93 L. 25   *Have you heard the argument?* It was sometimes customary when plays were presented before distinguished spectators to provide them with a written or printed synopsis of the plot.

P. 93 L. 30   *The Mouse-trap: marry how? Tropically*: figuratively; the First Quarto reads 'trapically', thereby indicating the pun.

P. 94 L. 2   *our withers are unwrung*: the withers are the part of the shoulder blade galled by the saddle. Hamlet says that of course this story need make neither himself nor the King touchy.

P. 94 L. 5   *You are a good Chorus*: the Chorus (called also the Prologue or Presenter) often appeared in Elizabethan plays to explain the action to the audience. Shakespeare seldom used a Chorus, but it is to be found in *II Henry IV, Henry V, Winter's Tale, Romeo and Juliet,* and *Pericles*.

P. 94 L. 6   *if I could see the puppets dallying*: Puppet shows were a primitive form of marionette which were popular in fairs and other gatherings. Whilst the puppet-master moved the strings he explained what was happening.

P. 94 L. 19   *Hecat's ban*: Hecate was the goddess of witch-craft.

P. 94 L. 31   *Give me some light*: This is the turning point of the play. Hamlet has proved the King guilty, and has also shown that he knows the truth about the murder. Hereafter the initiative passes to Claudius.

P. 95 L. 5   *a forest of feathers*: elaborate plumes affected by actors.

P. 95 L. 6   *Provincial roses*: rosettes.

fellowship in a cry of players: a full share in a com- P. 95 L. 7
pany of players; 'cry' is literally a pack of hounds.

choler: wrath; but Hamlet pretends that Guilden- P. 96 L. 2
stern means biliousness, the choleric temperament
being due to excess of bile.

pickers and stealers: fingers, appropriately used of P. 97 L. 1
Rosencrantz and Guildenstern because they were
trying to steal Hamlet's secrets from him.

recover the wind of me: come behind the game against P. 97 L. 13
the wind and so drive it into the net (toil).

fret: with the double meaning of (a) annoy, and P. 98 L. 5
(b) play on, as on the frets or bars of a guitar.

top of my bent: extreme limit – stretched to breaking P. 98 L. 18
point.

soul of Nero: Nero murdered his mother. Hamlet is P. 98 L. 30
now so bitterly stirred that he fears that he will lose
control of himself in his mother's presence.

To give them seals: to confirm a promise by fulfilling P. 99 L. 2
it, that is, 'lest my words lead me on to deeds'.

single and peculiar life: individual. This speech on the P. 99 L. 17
peculiar significance of the life of the sovereign
would have touched Shakespeare's audience. The
fear that anarchy would follow Queen Elizabeth's
death was very general.

primal eldest curse: the first curse, laid on Cain for the P. 100 L. 17
murder of his brother.

confront the visage of offence: stand directly in the way P. 100 L. 27
of.

limed: entangled in bird lime.   P. 101 L. 15

And so am I reveng'd: Hamlet is now apparently about P. 101 L. 23
to revenge his father. There naturally comes into his
mind the circumstance of the other murder, now to
be expiated; but the Ghost's most bitter complaint
was:

Cut off even in the blossoms of my sin,

Unhousel'd, disappointed, unaneled,
No reckoning made, but sent to my account
With all my imperfections on my head.
(p. 50, l. 28.)

To kill Claudius when his chances of salvation were greatest was therefore not revenge but benefit. To be satisfactory, revenge had to ensure hell fire for the victim. An example of thoroughly artistic revenge is to be found in Thomas Nashe's *Jack Wilton the Unfortunate Traveller*. Cutwolf wishing to exact vengeance on Esdras (who had murdered his brother) succeeds in cornering his victim. The victim in despair promises to commit any crime or blasphemy to save his life. Whereupon Cutwolf demanded 'First and foremost, he should renounce God and his laws, and utterly disclaim the whole title or interest he had in any covenant of salvation. Next, he should curse Him to his face, as Job was willed by his wife, and write an absolute firm obligation of his soul to the Devil, without condition or exception. Thirdly and lastly, (having done this), he should pray to God fervently never to have mercy upon him or pardon him ... These fearful ceremonies brought to an end, I bade him ope his mouth and gape wide. He did so, (as what will not slaves do for fear?); therewith made I no more ado, but shot him full into the throat with my pistol: no more spake he after; so did I shoot him that he might never speak after, or repent him. His body being dead looked as black as a toad: the Devil presently branded it for his own.'

Revenges almost as extravagant occur in such plays as *The Spanish Tragedy*, *Antonio's Revenge* (which is contemporary with *Hamlet*), and later in the tragedies of Webster and Tourneur.

P. 101 L. 26 *To Heaven*: the rest of the line is silent, as Hamlet

remembers the Ghost's words. Shakespeare's silences
are often most effective.

sets a blister: brands as a harlot.   P. 104 L. 6

thunders in the index: i.e. 'If there is so much noise in   P. 104 L. 15
the preliminary pages, what is to follow?

Counterfeit presentment: portrait. In modern perform-   P. 104 L. 17
ances Hamlet usually wears a miniature of his father,
while Gertrude wears a miniature of Claudius. In
the Eighteenth century, wall portraits were used.

Set his seal: guarantee.   P. 104 L. 24

Rebellious Hell ... fire: 'if the lust in a woman of   P. 105 L. 12
your age is uncontrollable, youth can have no re-
straining virtue.'

Compulsive ardour: compelling lust.   P. 105 L. 16

vice of Kings: the caricature of a King. The Vice was   P. 105 L. 32
the Clown in the old Morality plays.

Enter Ghost: The First Quarto reads *Enter the Ghost* P. 106 L. 4
in its night gown, i.e. dressing gown.

excrements: that which grows out of the body, hair   P. 106 L. 25
and nails.

either the devil: Some such word as 'quell' has been   P. 108 L. 11
omitted in the Quarto.

famous ape: The story evidently was about an ape   P. 109 L. 4
that thought to fly by jumping out of a birdcage. It
is not known.

try conclusions: repeat the experiment.   P. 109 L. 5

petar: a land mine for breaching walls and gates. P. 109 L. 19
Elizabethan military engineers were familiar with
trench warfare which had been much used in the
wars in France in 1591-1594.

Goodnight, mother: In the Second Quarto the scene P. 109 L. 29
ends here, and the next scene begins *Enter King and
Queen*, with *Rosencrantz and Guildenstern*, to whom
at line 4 the Queen says 'Bestow this place on us a
little while.' Stage direction and words are omitted

in the Folio, which continues the episode as one scene. The Act division, marked in modern texts, was first made in a quarto of 1676 and since followed by editors. It is wrong; for the scene does not end until p. 111, l. 27.

P. 110 L. 13   *brainish apprehension:* mad imagination.

P. 112 L. 24   *hide fox, and all after:* a children's game like hide and seek. With these words Hamlet gives his companions the slip and runs off.

P. 113 L. 1   *He's loved of the distracted multitude:* another echo of the Essex affair.

P. 113 L. 6   *Deliberate pause:* a plan thought out.

P. 113 L. 27   *variable service:* choice of dishes.

P. 115 L. 1   *cicatrice:* scar, wound barely healed. There is no trace of this incident in the play.

P. 115 L. 12   *Enter Fortinbras:* Fortinbras is briefly introduced here with his army in order that there shall be no need for explanation when he reappears at the end of the play.

P. 115 L. 16   *conveyance:* permission to convey.

P. 115 L. 19   *in his eye:* in his presence.

P. 115 L. 24   *Enter Hamlet, etc:* The rest of the scene is omitted in the Folio. The passage is topical. In 1601 Ostend was being defended by an Anglo-Dutch force under Sir Francis-Vere. In December the situation was critical, as Vere could only muster 1,200 fit men against 10,000 Spaniards. The Spaniards made a desperate assault which was repulsed with a loss of 2,000 dead and much material. Ostend, like Ypres in World War I, was defended rather as a symbol than for its military value, and the gallantry shown on both sides was much commented upon. Thus Camden: 'There was not in our age any siege and defence maintained with greater slaughter of men, nor continued longer. ... For the most warlike soldiers of the Low Coun-

tries, Spain, England, France, Scotland and Italy,
whilst they most eagerly contended for a barren plot
of sand, had as it were one common sepulchre, but
an eternal monument of their valour.'

large discourse: intelligence able to consider the future P. 116 L. 25
and the past.

IV. 5: The division of the Act should fall after Ham- P. 117
let's departure for England. The plot is developed in
three stages: (i) (Act I) how Hamlet learnt of the
murder of his father, (ii) (Act II–Act IV, Scene 4)
how he proved his uncle guilty but by the death of
Polonius became himself the victim of Polonius'
avenging son. (iii) (Act IV, Scene 4—the end) how
Laertes plotted to kill Hamlet, and how both sons
achieved vengeance. Between each episode there is
an interval of time suggested in the dialogue.

hearers to collection: causes them to make deductions. P. 118 L. 4

Enter Ophelia, distracted: The First Quarto reads P. 118 L. 17
*Enter Ophelia playing on a lute, and her hair down,
singing.*

cockle hat: pilgrims who had visited the Shrine of P. 118 L. 24
St James of Compostella wore a cockle shell in their
hats.

true-love showers: the tears of his faithful love. P. 119 L. 7

owl ... daughter: according to the legend Christ went P. 119 L. 9
into a baker's shop and asked for bread. The baker's
wife gave him a piece but was rebuked by her daughter for giving him too much. The daughter was
thereupon turned into an owl.

Saint Valentine's day: Feb. 14, the day when the P. 119 L. 15
birds are believed to mate. According to the legend
the first single man then seen by a maid is her destined
husband.

greenly: foolishly, as if we lacked ripe judgment. P. 120 L. 17

necessity ... beggar'd: i.e. not knowing the true facts. P. 120 L. 26

P. 120 L. 33   *Switzers:* Swiss body-guard.

P. 121 L. 3   *overpeering of his list:* coming over his boundary, i.e. flooding over the bands.

P. 122 L. 1   *There's such divinity doth hedge a King:* Spectators can hardly have failed to notice the parallel between this situation and what might have happened in Essex's rebellion, had he succeeded in breaking into White-hall Palace on 8th February, 1601. Queen Elizabeth was reported to have said, on hearing that Essex was winning, that He that placed her in that seat would preserve her in it, and that she wished to go with the troops against Essex 'to see if ever a rebel of them durst show their faces against her.'

P. 122 L. 29   *pelican:* The Quarto reading; the Folio has 'poli-tician'! The pelican was supposed to feed its young with its own blood.

P. 123 L. 15   *sends some precious instance of itself:* i.e. Ophelia has sent her sanity after Polonius.

P. 123 L. 26   *how the wheel becomes it:* variously explained as the 'refrain', or the 'spinning wheel' to which the song is sung. The likeliest explanation is that she breaks into a little dance at 'you must sing', and the 'wheel' is the circle as she turns on her toes.

P. 123 L. 29   *rosemary, that's for remembrance:* In the language of flowers Ophelia's gifts have their special meanings. Rosemary (remembrance) and pansies (thoughts) for her brother; fennel (flattery) and columbine (thanklessness) for the King; rue (sorrow) and a daisy (light o' love) for the Queen; violets (faithful-ness), for neither.

P. 125 L. 3   *hatchment:* the coats of arms of buckram carried in the funeral procession.

P. 125 L. 4   *formal ostentation:* ceremonious rites. In Shakespeare's time the funerals of great men were organized by the heralds and celebrated with much pomp and heraldic

ostentation. To bury Polonius 'hugger-mugger' was
thus an insult to the family.

too light for the bore of the matter: like a small shot in P. 126 L. 5
a cannon of large calibre words will fall short.

uncharge the practice: make no accusation of P. 128 L. 25
treachery.

the French ... well on horseback: The French horsemen P. 129 L. 11
at this time were famous.

in forgery of shapes and tricks: in imagination of what P. 129 L. 17
was possible for a horseman.

a pass of practice: treacherous thrust. P. 131 L. 5

drift look through ... not assay'd: 'better not attempt P. 131 L. 20
ithe plot if we should be betrayed by failure.'

There is a willow ... In the German *Fratricide Pun-* P. 132 L. 4
shed Ophelia throws herself over a cliff. 'In the winter after he (Shakespeare) was fifteen a girl of Tid-
dington, about a mile from Stratford, fell into the
water and was drowned where the Avon's banks in
summer are overhung by willows and thickly
crowned with wild flowers. He embalmed the memory of the place and the event in an elaborate dirge
for Ophelia ... It was not surprising that the story of
twenty years ago should have come to him, for the
girl's name was Katharine Hamlet.' (*Shakespeare at
Work*, p. 272.) There is a photograph of the spot in
E. I. Fripp's *Shakespeare Studies*, p. 136.

Christian burial: a suicide would rightfully be buried P. 133 L. 6
without Christian rites and in unsanctified ground.
The grave diggers (and later the priest) are profes-
sionally scandalized that Ophelia should be allowed
Christian burial solely because she is a lady of the
Court.

se offendendo: the Clown's Latin is astray, he means P. 133 L. 14
se defendendo, in self defence.

here lies the water ... own life: A similar argument was P. 133 L. 20

advanced in the celebrated case of Sir James Hales who drowned himself in 1554. As a suicide was a felon, his property was forfeited to the Crown. Hence the anxiety of his family to prove accident.

P. 134 L. 26   *unyoke:* finish the job – unyoking the oxen from the plough being the end of the day's work.

P. 135 L. 2   *get thee to Yaughan:* apparently a tavern keeper in the vicinity of the Globe Theatre.

P. 135 L. 5   *In youth when I.* ... The song which the Clown sings without much regard for sense or accuracy was first printed in *Tottel's Miscellany*, 1558.

P. 135 L. 13   *the hand of little employment hath the daintier sense:* i.e. those who are daintily brought up are the more sensitive.

P. 136 L. 2   *loggats:* a game in which billets of wood or bones were stuck in the ground and knocked over by throwing at them.

P. 136 L. 9   *quiddits ... indentures:* Hamlet strings out a number of legal terms natural to a lawyer. Quiddits (*subtle arguments*), quillets (*quibbles*), statutes (*bonds*), recognizances (*obligations*), fines (*conveyances*), voucher (*guarantor*), recoveries (*transfers*).

P. 136 L. 19   *pair of indentures:* A legal agreement was written in duplicate at either end of a piece of parchment which was then cut with a wavy or indented line. If any question of forgery was raised, both parts of the document could be fitted together.

P. 137 L. 12   *by the card:* Exactly. The card is the shipman's compass.

P. 137 L. 13   *equivocation:* The Jesuit doctrine of equivocation was much in the air at this time, and was denounced in various books put out in the autumn of 1601 by the secular Catholic priests who disliked the domination of the Jesuits.

P. 137 L. 15   *the toe of the peasant ... galls his kibe:* rubs his heel

into a blister. From about 1598 onwards writers
were becoming aware of certain social changes,
which are aptly summed up in *A health to the Gentlemanly profession of serving men* (entered 15th May,
1598). Yeomen farmers, grown rich by the profits
of the wars, sent their sons to London to learn fine
manners. Ben Jonson ridicules these upstart peasants
in Stephano in *Every Man in his Humour* (1598) and
Fungoso in *Every Man out of his Humour* (1599). The
sons of the new rich were conspicuous by their rustic
manners. Similarly the New Rich, profiteers of
World War I, were a constant subject for jest in the
1920's.

man and boy thirty years: Shakespeare apparently P. 138 L. 4
wishes to stress Hamlet's age, though the general
impression is that he was younger.

Enter bearers, etc: The stage directions in the early P. 139 L. 27
texts read: *Enter King, Queen, Laertes and the corse*
(Second Quarto); *Enter King, Queen, Laertes, and a
coffin, with Lords attendant* (Folio); *Enter King and
Queen, Laertes and other Lords, with a Priest after the
coffin* (Pirated Quarto). The modern stage direction
*Enter priests, etc., in procession ... King, Queen, their
trains,* etc misses the whole significance of the
'maimed rites'. In the speech headings of the Quarto
Priest is labelled *Doct,* which leads one critic to assume
that Shakespeare intended a Protestant Clergyman;
but the theology of the whole play is Catholic, and
a Protestant doctor would not encourage a requiem
and prayers for the dead. Moreover Laertes calls
him 'churlish priest'.

great command ... order: i.e. the King's command has P. 140 L. 6
overruled the proper procedure.

Pelion ... Olympus: when the giants fought the gods, P. 141 L. 3
they tried to reach heaven by piling Mount Pelion

on Mount Ossa. Mount Olympus where the Gods lived is the highest mountain in Greece.

P. 142 L. 10 *couplets:* young. The dove lays two eggs at a sitting.

P. 142 L. 23 *living monument:* with a double meaning (a) a lifelike status of the dead (b) the sacrifice of Hamlet.

P. 143 L. 3 *mutines in the bilboes:* mutineers in irons.

P. 143 L. 20 *bugs:* a word which has diminished in significance; in Shakespeare's time it meant goblins.

P. 143 L. 33 *baseness to write fair:* Elizabethan noblemen were taught in boyhood to write a fair ornamental hand which soon degenerated. Queen Elizabeth herself in her earliest letters wrote a beautiful script. Her letters as Queen are as difficult to decipher as any.

P. 145 L. 5 *to quit … comes here:* These lines are omitted in the Quarto.

P. 145 L. 21 *water-fly:* a little creature that flits about.

P. 145 L. 32 *bonnet to his right use:* Etiquette demanded that the inferior should stand with his head uncovered before the superior; hence Osric's embarrassment when Hamlet wishes him to be covered.

P. 146 L. 12 *believe me an absolute gentleman:* Osric, as the perfect little courtier, speaks the fashionable jargon of the day, which was too too ornate. Lodge (in *Wit's Misery*) mocked this affectation, giving as an example of arrogant verbiage the courtier who says 'My diminutive and defective slave, give me the coverage of my corpse to ensconce my person from frigidity,' when he means 'Boy, bring my cloak.'

P. 146 L. 13 *excellent differences:* excellencies peculiar to himself.

P. 146 L. 15 *card or calendar of gentry:* i.e. 'the very fashion plate of what a gentleman should be!'

P. 146 L. 18 *his definement:* Hamlet answers Osric in his own language and with so much more extravagant fluency that Osric is reduced almost to silence.

divide him inventorially: make a catalogue of his P. 146 L. 19
qualities.

semblable is his mirror: nothing is like him but his P. 146 L. 24
reflection.

edified by the margent: i.e. 'You need the notes to P. 147 L. 23
understand the text.'

lapwing ... on his head: the lapwing is so lively that P 148 L. 19
it runs as soon as hatched, hence *lapwing:* forward
creature.

comply with his dug: be ceremonious with his mother's P. 148 L. 21
breast.

fond and winnowed opinions: silly opinions as light as P. 148 L. 26
chaff.

brother: the Quarto reading. The Folio reads P. 150 L. 13
'mother', which may be correct.

my terms of Honour: Laertes will not commit himself P. 150 L. 16
to more than accepting Hamlet's apology 'without
prejudice'.

elder masters: experts. P. 150 L. 18

Stick fiery: stand out brightly. P. 150 L. 29

this pearl is thine: with these words Claudius drops P. 151 L. 31
the poisoned pearl into the cup.

make a wanton of me: mock me. P. 152 L. 19

In scuffling: The duel was with rapier and dagger. P. 152 L. 24
Hamlet closes, engaging Laertes' dagger with his
rapier. He drops the dagger in his left hand and
seizes the hilt of Laertes' rapier, forcing it back-
wards. Laertes must retaliate by a similar movement,
which leaves the combatants daggerless and with
each other's rapiers. The Elizabethan duel was far
less dignified and formal than a modern fencing-
match: it was quite within the rules to hamstring
one's opponent with the edge, or to cut him in
the forehead so that he was blinded with his own
blood.

P. 154 L. 8   *antique Roman:* like Cato or Brutus who committed
suicide when their cause was lost.

P. 154 L. 29   *occurrents ... solicited:* the circumstances which give
him my vote.

P. 155 L. 8   *quarry cries on havoc:* the heap of slain betokens a
pitiless slaughter.

P. 156 L. 10   *Let four captains:* It is usual in Shakespeare's tragedies
for someone to pronounce a brief epitaph over the
dead. The last word on Hamlet is that he was a
soldier.

P. 156 L. 16   *take up the body:* The Second Quarto reads 'bodies'.
On the stage presumably the King, the Queen and
Laertes die within the inner stage, and their bodies
are hidden by the curtain, thereby leaving only
Hamlet's body to be carried away ceremoniously.

GLOSSARY

abridgement: pastime.

additional: honour.

admiration: wonder, astonishment.

aery: nest.

affection: affection.

anchor: anchorite, hermit.

amble: walk affectedly.

angle: rod and line.

annexment: attachment.

antic disposition: pretended madness.

appurtenance: that which belongs to.

argument: plot of a play.

arras: tapestry hanging.

arter: artery.

at point exactly: at all points, complete.

barr'd: thwarted.

bated: abated.

bedded: lying flat.

beetles: juts.

beshrew: plague on.

bespeak: command.

beteem: allow.

bisson: blind.

blank: target.

blown youth: youth in full bloom.

bodkin: dagger.

bodykins: little body.

bourne: boundary.

brainish: mad.

braz'd: covered with brass.

breath: utterance.

breathing time: time for exercise.

brokers: go-betweens.

buttons: buds.

buz, buz: stale news.

canon: law.

canopy: covering.

canker: maggot.

cap-a-pe: from head to foot.

capable: capable of feeling.

cataplasm: plaster.

cautel: craft.

censure: opinion.

chapless: without cheeks.

character: (a) handwriting. (b) write.

chough: jackdaw.

clepe: call.

climature: climate, country.

coil: turmoil.

collateral: related, accessory.

comply with: use ceremony with.

compost: manure.

conceit: imagination.
compounded: mixed.
condolement: lamentation.
conjunctive: inseparable.
consequence: sequel.
consummation: conclusion.
continent: able to contain.
contraction: contract of marriage.
convoy: means of conveyance.
coped: encountered.
coted: came alongside.
couch: lie down.
cousin: kinsman.
counter: follow the scent in the wrong direction.
counterfeit presentment: portrait.
crowner: coroner.

Danskers: Danes.
declension: downward path.
discourse of reason: power of reason.
distemper'd: disturbed.
dole: grief.
distilled: melted.
distract: out of her mind.
doublet: short, close-fitting coat.
doubt: suspect.
douts: puts out.
down-gyved: hanging like fetters round his ankles.
drift of question: indirect inquiry.

drossy: scummy.
dupped: opened.

ecstasy: madness.
effects: material advantages.
eisel: vinegar.
emulate: emulous, jealous.
enactures: resolutions.
encompassments: circumlocution.
encumbered: folded.
entertainment: welcome hospitality.
entreatments: preliminary conversations.
escoted: paid.
espiels: spies.
even: straight.
even Christian: fellow Christian.
extent: outward show.
extorted: evilly acquired.
extravagant: wandering.
eyases: hawks.

faction: party.
fantasy: imagination, illusion.
fardels: burdens.
fat: out of condition.
favour: face, appearance.
fay: faith.
feats: acts.
fellies: rim of a wheel.
flats: low-lying shore.
flushing: filling with water.

fordo: destroy.
foreknowing: foreknowledge.
forms: mental images.
free: guiltless.
fretted: ornamented.
friending: friendliness.
function: action, behaviour.
fust: grow musty.

gaged: pledged.
gate: bitterness.
gain-giving: misgiving.
gait: progress.
general gender: the people at large.
generous: of gentle birth.
gentry: gentlemanly behaviour.
germane: relative.
gib: tomcat.
God buy: God be with.
God 'ild you: God reward you.
gorge: throat.
grizzled: grey.
gross and scope: full view.
gules: red in the jargon of heraldry.
gulf: whirlpool.
gyves: fetters.

habit: garments.
hangers: straps for carrying the sword.
happily: haply.
harrows: distresses.
hearsed: buried.

heat: anger.
hebenon: probably henbane.
hectic: fever.
hic et ubique: here and everywhere.
honest: chaste.
hoodman blind: blind man's buff.
hugger-mugger: 'anyhow', i.e. in secret haste.
husbandry: economy.
Hyperion: the Sun.
Hyrcanian beast: the tiger.

idle: silly.
Ilium: the citadel of Troy.
impasted: encrusted.
imponed: pawned, bet.
imposthume: a boil.
impress: conscription.
incorps'd: of one body with.
incorrect to: unruled by.
inhibition: prohibition.
infants: buds.
instances: motives.
inurned: buried.
investments: outward garments.
it: its.

jig: dance wantonly.
jointress: partner.
journeyman: hired workman.
jowls: claps down.
jump: immediately.
just: exactly.

keep: live.
kettle: kettle drum.
kindless: unnatural.

larded: garnished.
large discourse: power of reasoning.
lazar-like: like leprosy.
lenten: fasting, meagre.
lets: hinders.
liberal conceit: elaborate pattern.
lighted: alighted.
loose: torn loose.
luxury: lust.

made probation: proved to be true.
mazzard: pate.
meed: merit.
merely: utterly.
miching mallecho: slinking mischief.
milch: moist.
mobled: muffled.
moiety competent: adequate share.
mope: be dull.
moth: mote, speck of dust.
mouse: a term of affection.
mows: insulting grimaces.
murdering-pieces: cannon loaded with grape-shot.

nave: centre of a wheel.

nonce: for the once, occasion.
occulted: concealed.
o'erraught: overtook.
o'er-sized: painted over.
o'er-teemed: exhausted by bearing children.
omen: disaster.
operant: active.
opposite: obstacle.
overpeering of his list: overstepping its boundary.
outstretched: exaggerated.

paddock: toad.
painted: motionless as in a picture.
painting: imitation.
pajock: peacock.
pales: defences.
pall: fail.
passages of proof: experiences that prove.
performed at height: achieved greatly.
peak: mope.
pioner: engineer, or military miner.
plausive: pleasing.
pith: marrow.
plurisy: excess.
policy: state craft.
porpentine: porcupine.
posset: curdle.
powers: forces.
precurse: forerunner.

pregnant: ready, apt.

prenominate: aforesaid.

prescripts: commands.

presently: immediately.

pressure: impression, imprint of a seal.

prevent: forestall.

primy nature: nature in its spring time.

process: procedure.

property of easiness: a matter of indifference.

pursy: puffy.

quaintly: skilfully.

quality: acting profession.

quit: repay.

quoted: noted.

rack: the cloud in the sky.

range: run about.

rank: overgrown.

ranker: richer.

razed: ornamented with cuts.

r each: far sight.

recorder: a wood-wind instrument.

reechy: grimy.

remorse: pity.

replication: echo.

resolve: melt.

respect: consideration.

responsive to: matching well.

retrograde: contrary.

rhapsody: meaningless sound.

rheum: moisture.

riband: ribbon.

rivals: partners.

romage: literally, clearing out the hold of a ship.

rouse: deep draught, carouse.

row: line.

sable: black.

sallets: piquancies.

sanctified: sanctimonious.

saws: wise sayings.

school: university.

scrimers: fencers.

sealed: confirmed the election.

season: (a) qualify, (b) ripen.

secure hour: hour of ease.

seized of: possessed of.

sensible: perceived by the senses.

shark'd up: collected indiscriminately.

sheeted: shrouded.

shent: rebuked.

shoon: shoes.

siege: seat, and so rank, importance.

sold in fee: freehold.

sort: (a) fall out, (b) reckon.

sounds: swoons.

splenitive: hot tempered.

springe: snare.

stamp of nature: the impression made by nature: natural character.

station: noble bearing.

statists: statesmen.

still: ever, continuously.

stithy: smithy.

stomach: requiring courage.

stoup: large drinking cup.

stuck: thrust.

subject: subjects.

sullies (spelt *sallies* in the Second Quarto): blemishes.

suppliance of a minute: momentary.

supposed: estimation.

Switzers: Swiss body-guard.

Swounds: by God's wounds.

taints: blemishes.

takes: bewitches.

tarre on: set on.

tax'd · censured.

temple: i.e. the body.

tempered: mixed.

tend: attend.

tender: (a) offer, (b) counter.

tent: probe.

touch'd: implicated.

tricked: heraldic word for painted.

umbrage: shadow.

unbated: unblunted, sharp.

unction: ointment.

uneffectual: made powerless.

unfortified: irreligious.

ungracious: graceless.

unimproved: unschooled, rash.

union: pearl.

unpregnant: having no living thought within.

unproportioned: unsuitable.

unreclaimed: untouched, naturally wild.

unsifted: untried.

unsinew'd: nerveless.

up-spring: a wild dance.

vailed: lowered.

valanced: fringed, i.e. with a beard.

variable: varied.

varnish: gloss.

ventages: stops in the recorder.

vigour: violent action.

voice: vote.

windlasses: winding about.

yaw: sail unsteadily.

yesty collection: frothy knowledge.

PENGUIN POPULAR CLASSICS

Published or forthcoming

Louisa M. Alcott	Little Women
Jane Austen	Emma
	Mansfield Park
	Northanger Abbey
	Persuasion
	Pride and Prejudice
	Sense and Sensibility
Anne Brontë	Agnes Grey
	The Tenant of Wildfell Hall
Charlotte Brontë	Jane Eyre
	Shirley
	Villette
Emily Brontë	Wuthering Heights
John Buchan	The Thirty-Nine Steps
Lewis Carroll	Alice's Adventures in Wonderland
	Through the Looking Glass
John Cleland	Fanny Hill
Wilkie Collins	The Moonstone
	The Woman in White
Joseph Conrad	Heart of Darkness
	Lord Jim
	Nostromo
	The Secret Agent
	Victory
James Fenimore Cooper	The Last of the Mohicans
Stephen Crane	The Red Badge of Courage
Daniel Defoe	Moll Flanders
	Robinson Crusoe
Charles Dickens	Bleak House
	The Christmas Books Volume I
	David Copperfield
	Great Expectations
	Hard Times
	Little Dorrit
	Nicholas Nickleby
	Oliver Twist
	The Pickwick Papers
	A Tale of Two Cities